DANCING THROUGH LIFE
BOOK SEVEN

Lyrical
DANCE

PATRICIA M. ROBERTSON

Chapter 1

Esther tilted her head slightly to smell the corsage still fastened to her lapel. She leaned back into the car seat, stared out into the darkness of her neighborhood in Cascade Falls and sighed, "It was a good day."

Peter glanced over at Esther and touched her arm. "You doing okay?"

"Just tired." She smiled as she remembered the events of the day.

The impossible had happened. Kathleen had gotten married. And to a minister, no less, to Pastor Joe. Had it really happened, or was it a dream that would disappear with the dawn? This miracle had been in the making for over forty years. Sometimes God took God's time, but then God comes through in ways Esther would never have imagined. Such as bringing her wild child, Kathleen, safely home.

If only Kathleen's dad could have been here to witness the event. Dale would have been proud. Esther looked over at Peter, the outline of his face barely visible in the dark car. Only married for five years, yet it felt like a lifetime. It was hard to remember when he hadn't been a part of her life. But there had been years, many years, over fifty, before he had come into her life. There had been Dale, and a long stretch of raising her kids alone, and then raising her grandsons. Still she couldn't imagine a time without Peter. He had become such an integral, essential, part of her life. She knew the lines on his face, the angle of his shoulders as he entered a room and quickly took stock of the situation. He didn't slip in unannounced like some, sliding into the shadows or corners. No, he didn't need an announcement. He entered a room and took command, his presence going before him.

She knew the thickness of his neck and chest and the roundness of his belly, expanding from too many beers. Peter would never be anyone's project, though he did need taking care of. First there was his cholesterol … She wanted him to be around for a long time.

She felt safe in his presence. She was happy by his side. She didn't mind the role of side-kick. Rather, she relished it, reveling in the thought that he was hers and she was his, to have and to hold. Just like Kathleen had someone in her life now, too. Something Esther thought would never happen.

No, she didn't need to be center-stage. She was happier on the side-line. The invisible hands that made everything happen, that raise children, bandage booboos, warm hot chocolate on a cold winter night and tuck into bed with a kiss. She was the one cheering on the others in her life. That was what she did. She didn't need acclaim or recognition. All she needed was to feel appreciated by those closest to her. That was enough for her.

She winced as she was struck with a sudden sharp pain in her head.

Peter reached over and took her hand. "Something wrong?"

"Headache. I'll take something for it when I get home." Her head throbbed. The worst headache in the world, she thought. But she wouldn't tell Peter that. No need to worry him. Probably just the excitement and stress of the day catching up to her.

Peter squeezed her hand, let go and gripped the steering wheel as he turned into their driveway.

"Home." He turned off the car and looked over at her. "Time to get you to bed." The tenderness in his voice broke through the throbbing in her head. Yes, he was a good one. Just like Dale. She had been blessed to have two loves in her life.

2

"*Whatever you say*," she wanted to tell him, but the words wouldn't form in her mouth. Something was wrong. The last words she heard was Peter calling her name.

"Esther, Esther …"

Chapter 2

Kathleen cuddled up next to Joe, allowing the warmth of his body to envelop her, breathing in the scent of his form. All she wanted was here, lying by her side. No kids, no shame. She had never thought she could be so happy. Who'd have thought a ring and a vow would make such a difference. Who'd have thought she could be so in love. If only this night would last forever.

She'd slept with men before, that was common knowledge. God knows, her sons were not miraculous births. But this was different. She was glad for the dry spell, the self-imposed time-out from sex. She had needed the time to recover, become a better version of her earlier self. What they'd said in Twelve-Step programs was true: relationships are where you test your recovery. Most recommend two years of sobriety before getting into a serious relationship. She had thought it all nonsense back then, back when she had attended court-ordered AA meetings. She hadn't thought she had learned anything, but apparently, she had as bits of Twelve-Step wisdom popped into her head.

It had taken her a long time to be ready for a relationship, but it had been worth the wait. Joe was more than she could have hoped for, more than she had dreamed about. She didn't deserve such happiness, and yet here she was, wrapped in his arms, a married woman. No one would have thought it, least of all, her.

They had made a commitment, before God and family. She could even forgive the fact that he was a minister. So he wasn't perfect. She could deal with that. She curled in closer.

They were spending the night at a hotel not far from the Detroit airport. Their flight wasn't until later that morning, but Kathleen had not wanted to spend her first night as a married woman in the church manse. There would be time enough to do that once they returned from their honeymoon. She had already moved her clothes. What few remaining belongings she had, she would move when she got back. It wasn't as if she had a lot to move. Living in her mom's basement, she hadn't needed much.

The phone rang. Already! She had been warned about this from other spouses of pastors, late-night phone calls from church members in crisis. "Just ignore it, Joe," she mumbled. "Who would call on our wedding night? Can't you have even one night off?"

"Kathleen, it's your phone."

Her phone? How could that be possible? Who would be calling her now?

Chapter 3

Pain, sharp, staggering pain hitting her between her eyeballs, swelling her head. Why can't she move? Why won't her tongue form words?

"Whaaa?" she tried to get the word out. Where was she? Sounds of beeping, antiseptic smells, a curtain pulled partway around her bed. Was she at the hospital? A young man in a smock poked her, inserting a needle. A woman in a white coat prodded her, asked her questions. She had to get off of this hard bed. Had to get home. She was needed at home. What was going on? Kathleen's wedding? Was that today, or days ago?

The woman held up her finger and asked her to follow it. It hurt to move her head. It hurt when she didn't move it. Why do they keep asking her questions?

"Whaaa?" Why? She tried to form words but they came out wrong. Why couldn't she say the right word?

Peter stood beside her bed and calmly answered each question. How can he be so calm? He should be screaming for answers, making sounds she couldn't make. Beneath the calm surface she knew he wasn't so calm, but he would never let on to anyone, even her. She just knew it from the tightness in his lips, the tiredness in his eyes.

"Don't worry. It'll be okay," Peter answered her unspoken question. "The doctors think you've had a stroke. They are asking questions to determine where the damage is and the nature of the stroke," he reassured her. "They need to know that to treat you."

She wanted to scream at him. Do something, anything. Get her out of here. But she was also relieved to know he was there, taking care of matters, taking care of her. ... A stroke? She couldn't have a stroke? Why was her right arm so weak? Why couldn't she feel her right leg? This couldn't be happening.

"They're going to take you for a cat-scan," Peter told her. One of the smock-clad young men started pushing her bed down the hallway.

She tried to grab Peter's hand but her right arm lay limp at her side. Peter put his hand on her shoulders and walked alongside her.

"Don't worry. I'm here. I'll be here when you get out."

Don't leave me.

Kathleen had been surprised to see Peter's name come up on her cell phone. She knew it had to be serious for him to call her.

"Your mom would kill me if she knew I called you, …"

Mom, what could be wrong with mom? Her stomach churned. She sat up in bed, immediately wide awake, wanting to shout out, cry out as Peter continued to spew out words she didn't understand.

"… but she's in no shape to do that, whereas I know you would kill me if I didn't call." Was he trying to make a joke? How could he? Peter's feeble attempt at humor didn't fool her. His voice was strained, pretend calm.

"What's wrong?" the words came out calmer than she felt. Inside she was screaming, but on the surface her calm matched that of Peter's.

"I'm so sorry to disturb you like this."

"Peter, what's wrong? Has there been an accident? Is she okay?"

"Your Mom. Something's wrong. They think she had a stroke."

"But she's okay, right?"

"For now. They are going to run more tests in the morning. They are keeping her for observation."

"We'll be right there." Kathleen flung her legs over the side of the bed and stood up.

"No, don't come. Your mom would hate it if she thought you interrupted your honeymoon for her. There's nothing you can do. I just wanted you to know."

"We'll be there," Kathleen insisted and hung up. "There's something wrong with Mom," was all she said. Joe was already up and getting dressed. They checked out and loaded their luggage.

Who would have thought that she would be the one with an emergency affecting their ability to get away?

"I'm sorry," she stated as they drove through the dark. "I just have to see her, know that she's okay. We might still have time to make our flight."

"No need to apologize. Of course, we have to see your mom. If we have to, we can reschedule for a later flight."

Here she was, her wedding night, and she was spending it at the hospital. She hated the hospital, she thought as Joe drove. She wanted to get there as fast as possible, reassure herself that her mom was okay, then get back to her honeymoon.

"Can't you drive faster? Run that red light. There's no one around. This is an emergency."

"We'll get there," Joe reassured her. She wasn't reassured.

She hadn't eaten much at the reception, but what she had was churning in her stomach, ready to explode. She had moved back home nine years ago, straight from her stint in jail. She had arrived with only a back-pack. Outside of clothing, she hadn't accumulated much else. She had slept in the bed her mom had provided, eaten food her mom bought and cooked, lived in the home her mom had kept since her dad's death when she was four. She owed her mom everything. How could this be happening?

"We spend way too much time at the hospital," Kathleen complained. Her anger kept her fears at bay.

"It will be all right." Joe reached for her hand. She pulled her hand away.

"How can you say that? You don't know."

"No, I don't know, but imagining the worst won't make it any different. We'll find out when we get there. Whatever the situation, we'll get through it together."

"All the more reason to drive faster." How could he be so calm?

"It won't help if we get in an accident on the way. We don't want to arrive in an ambulance."

"Very funny, Pastor," she stated, yet somehow his humor helped her breathe.

"I'm not trying to be funny, just trying to calm my wife down." Wife, the word sounded both strange and endearing. Was she really a wife?

Kathleen released her crossed arms, allowing them to slip to her side. They rode in silence for a while before she spoke. "Some honeymoon. Spending it in the hospital."

"We don't know yet. We may still be able to go on our honeymoon."

"How could you even suggest that I leave when my mom is in the hospital." And yet that was precisely what Kathleen was hoping to do. She thought back over all of their plans.

A honeymoon had not been in their budget. Kathleen was not paid a lot as the director of a non-profit, and Joe not much more as a minister. One of Joe's church members had offered to give them a week at his timeshare in the Bahamas as a wedding gift. Other church members had chipped in to pay for their flight. Since they did not need to furnish a new home, others gave them gifts of cash to be spent on the honeymoon.

"There are some perks to being a pastor," Joe had said when he told her about the gifts.

"There should be for all of the negatives involved."

Joe had refused to accept the bait, avoiding the argument. They had already had too many "discussions" about what it meant to marry a pastor.

She did appreciate the perks and had been looking forward to a week on the beach, just Joe and her. How quickly plans can change. All it takes is a phone call.

Peter met them outside of ICU where her mom had been moved. "She's sleeping comfortably," Peter told them as they hugged. "The doctor said that's common in cases of strokes. Sleep is good. It takes a lot out of a person, leaves them exhausted."

"Can we see her?" Joe asked.

"You can but there's not much you can do. There's no reason for you to miss your honeymoon. There will be plenty for you to do when you get back."

Kathleen remembered saying similar words to her mom back when Grandpop had fallen and broken his hip. Her mom and Peter had been on an extended vacation. At the time, the words had made sense to her. With Peter's help, they had been able to convince her mom not to come home early. Now those words seemed hollow. What a stupid thing to say. How could she leave when her mom needed her?

"I have to see her," Kathleen said and walked past Peter. Dale, Kathleen's brother, was sitting next to her bed.

"Hey, sis." Dale offered his chair to Kathleen and pulled another alongside hers.

"She looks okay," Kathleen said. There were no droopy eyelids or melting face that she associated with a stroke. "Are you sure it's a stroke?"

"The doctors will know more after they do more tests. Sometimes it's a matter of ruling out other possibilities. It also depends on what part of the brain is affected but they're pretty sure. They've already given her TPA to prevent further damage," Dale explained.

"Pretty sure, pretty sure. That's not enough. Don't they have to be certain before they start giving her drugs?" Kathleen looked at all of the monitors on her mom. She wanted to rip them off of her and take her home.

"Right now, the doctors say the best thing we can do for her is let her rest. So you see there's no reason you can't go on your honeymoon," Peter said.

"No one is going on a honeymoon, not when my mom is hooked up to a machine. Stop suggesting it." Only an hour ago, on the drive over, she had been certain that was what she wanted. She would make sure her mom was okay, then be on her way. Now she wanted to strangle Peter for even suggesting it.

"Let me have some time with her," Kathleen demanded. Dale stood up. Peter looked like he was about to protest when Joe nodded his head at the door and escorted them out so his bride could have this time with her mother.

Kathleen leaned in, stroking her mom's arm, willing her to open her eyes. "Mom, I don't know what's going on inside that head of yours, but if you can hear me, let me know, give me a sign." Kathleen waited for a sign, any movement, a finger, or a twitch of her lip, anything. Nothing.

That was how her stomach felt, nothing, empty. How could her mom lay there and not respond? Her mom always responded to her, even if Kathleen didn't like what her mother had to say. This was not her mom. How could she leave her like this, hanging onto the edge of a cliff, dangling, not knowing the outcome? Her mom was dangling, and so was she. No, there was no way she would leave now. No way she could leave.

She saw the men sitting together in the family waiting room. She would have to convince them. Joe would be on her side. He had the most to lose, either way. She knew he wouldn't go against her in such an important decision even if it meant losing out on their honeymoon. Dale wouldn't fight her either. He knew not to get in her way when her mind was made up. Peter was the problem. He could put up a fuss, but what would that do? He couldn't force her to leave, any more than anyone could force her to do something she didn't want to do. It was time Peter learned that. He wasn't going to stand between her and her mother.

"I can't leave her, not like this," she announced before anyone could say a word.

"Kathleen, if she was alert, what would she say?" Peter asked as he stood up. "What good is your missing your honeymoon?"

"She'd say to get out of here. But I can't go. You understand, don't you, Joe?" Joe stood up and wrapped his arm around her in support.

"Of course, we'll stay here until your mom is better."

Peter ignored what Joe said. "Kathleen, what do you need to happen to get you to leave?" Peter asked. "I don't mean to go away. I mean to feel free to go enjoy your honeymoon."

Kathleen focused on a spot across the room and thought deeply. She knew what she needed. "I need to know she's going to be okay." Her voice started to crack, then she strengthened it. "That I will be able to talk to her again."

"Kathleen, you know this is what Mom would have wanted. You can't do anything here. Go, enjoy your honeymoon and come back well rested," Dale joined the conversation. How could he say that?

"How can you take Peter's side in this?"

"There's no side, Kathleen." Peter said. "We all want what's best for you and for your mom."

Kathleen glanced at Joe, her lone support. They were making sense. She was the one who wasn't making sense. But how could she enjoy a honeymoon knowing her mom may be in a semi-coma state? What if she didn't wake up? Or if she woke up and she wasn't there?

"I have to see her again," Kathleen said and walked out of the room, followed by the rest.

This time when Kathleen sat down next to her and spoke to her, her mother opened her eyes. When she saw Kathleen, at first there was nothing, no sign of recognition. Then a glint of remembrance. Her mother became animated. She was trying to speak, but the words were garbled. "No ..." finally came out.

"It's okay, Mom. It's me, Kathleen. I'll stay with you. You're going to be okay." Her mother became more agitated. She looked at Peter.

"I think she's trying to tell you something," Peter said.

Kathleen could tell it too, but she didn't want to accept it.

"I'm not going anywhere, Mom. I'm staying here." The more Kathleen insisted, the more her mother struggled to speak. Her mom's eyes locked into Peter's eyes, trying to tell him what Kathleen refused to acknowledge.

"No," her mother said. "No," she repeated and shook her head.

"I think you better leave, Kathleen. This is not good for your mom. She needs her rest."

"Go," the word came out, slow, drawn-out.

"Okay, I'll go back to the waiting room until she has more sleep."

"No, I think you need to leave, go on your honeymoon. I think that's what your mom is trying to say, isn't it, honey?" Kathleen saw how Peter gazed at her mom. They were speaking without words, her mom's eyes saying everything he needed to know. Tears flowed down her mom's cheeks as her eyes told him what her mouth couldn't. Kathleen saw it, too. She saw the glance that passed between them. Then her mom looked at her, willing her to understand what she couldn't say. "Go," she repeated.

"Okay, Mom," tears spilled off Kathleen's eyelashes and onto her cheeks. "You and Peter win this time. I'm going on my honeymoon but it won't be as easy to get rid of me next time," Kathleen forced a smile and kissed her mom on her cheek before leaving.

Chapter 4

Her grandmother tried to turn in the hospital bed. The sheets rustled as her right arm flopped by her side. Ashley sat in a chair not far from the bed, looking at her phone. She put down her phone and examined her grandmother. Was Grandma trying to say something?

"Grandma." She came to her side. "Are you okay?"

Grandma stared at her like she didn't know who she was.

"It's me, Ashley." Ashley moved closer.

There was a glimmer of remembrance. Her grandmother tried to smile but her mouth didn't work. She could barely curl the corners of her lips. She tried to talk. What Ashley heard came as if from someone else, not her grandmother.

"Grandma, you've had a stroke. The night of Aunt Kathleen's wedding. Do you remember?"

Grandma struggled to respond. She looked tired from the effort. Her grandma fought to form the question, "How long?"

"It's been a couple of days, Grandma. You've been sleeping a lot."

"Oh," her eyes said, then shut.

Sleep is good, Ashley thought. That was what her dad had told her. He told her to let Grandma sleep and not be surprised if she didn't remember her. But how could Grandma not remember her? How could anyone not remember her, but especially Grandma? It just wasn't like her grandmother.

Ashley went back to her phone. It was her turn to keep vigil. She had decided to at no one's prompting. She wanted to be here. But it was boring. At least she had her phone and social media. You were supposed to be sixteen to visit in the stroke unit, but she slipped past the vigilant eyes of the nursing staff without a second look. At fifteen, it was easier for her to pass as older. Her sister, Grace, hadn't been as

14

successful. When Grace tried to stay with Grandma, she had been told to leave.

"But Ashley …" she started to say. Ashley had cut her off with a glance. Grace knew better than to reveal her sister's age to the guardian of the stroke ward. Grace had left with her dad, brother and step-mother while Ashley had stayed behind.

Ashley texted her friends. "Band practice tonight?"

"Y," Caleb responded.

"Where?"

"Your place?"

"Will ask my dad." Ashley was grateful for the diversion.

Her grandmother dozed in and out of consciousness. Ashley wanted to be here, yet she didn't. She felt grown-up and responsible, taking her turn staying with her grandma. But she also remembered her mom, how she had been in and out of consciousness the last weeks of her life. She didn't like the memory – but it came. This was atonement. She had not sat with her mom. It had been too hard. So now she was sitting with her grandma.

It wasn't the same.

Chapter 5

Kathleen sat at the kitchen table drinking her morning coffee. She had reluctantly agreed to move into the manse when married. Much as she had wanted to return to Cascade Falls and see how her mother was doing, she hated the thought of returning to the manse after their honeymoon. She had loved the time with Joe, lying on the beach, but the quiet just gave her mind more time to worry. Once she stepped over the threshold of this turn-of-the-century building, the honeymoon was clearly over. They couldn't afford to buy a house and it didn't make sense to rent a place when they had a perfectly good home that would have sat empty if Joe moved out. So, she had agreed. And there were perks. There was the housekeeper. Kathleen had no problem relinquishing that responsibility. But then there were all those church members who considered the manse an extension of the church. And the church meetings.

Time to start her day. Kathleen put her coffee cup in the sink and headed back through the house, where she surprised a group of seven women, all appearing to be in their sixties or above, sitting in their living room. Three on the couch, two on the loveseat and the other two in the remaining seats, drinking coffee and munching on Danish. Was that her cups and dishes? They must have taken them from the side cabinet in the dining room, where a partially empty coffee pot was perched, the stale odor of coffee starting to fill the room.

"It's so much more comfy meeting here than in the church hall," a woman with a bob ala Hillary Clinton said. "Pastor doesn't mind. You don't mind, do you?"

Kathleen stood with her mouth partially open as she struggled to come up with a response, one that would be appropriately polite, as befitting a pastor's wife.

"We're the Women's Mission Guild. Would you like to join us?" another with dyed auburn hair in soft curls asked before Kathleen answered the first question. Kathleen was relieved at the reprieve.

"Oh, no … no, thank you. I'll just get out of your way." Kathleen slipped back into the kitchen where she remained captive until the meeting ended, and the ladies brought their coffee cups and plates into the kitchen.

"We'll wash these and get out of your way," they told her.

"It will get better," Joe stated that night over dinner. "You just have to set boundaries. Once church members realize you aren't going to be involved in all of the church committees, they'll stop asking." Joe took a bite of his chicken casserole. "Hmmm. Good. Yours?"

"No. Mrs. Whitmore brought it by this morning."

Joe nodded his head in approval and dug in.

There had been a steady flow of visitors to the manse, asking how she was adjusting and inviting her to attend meetings and lead groups. And then there were the casseroles. Word must have gotten out about her lack of ability in the kitchen. Couldn't let their pastor suffer from his wife's cooking.

"But what about meetings in our living room?"

"I'll talk to the mission guild," Joe assured her. She and Joe had talked about this before getting engaged. They had an understanding. Now, she needed a similar understanding with the church members.

Kathleen had wanted a simple wedding with just immediate family: her kids, her mom and Peter, her brother, Dale, and his family, Joe's kids and parents. That would have been enough for her, but not for the church.

"We have to tell the church sometime," Joe had told her.

"Why can't we just elope and tell them afterwards?" They had argued. Joe had won this fight. Kathleen realized he was right. She would have to find a way of relating to Joe's congregation eventually. Why start out on a negative? She already knew church members, so why should it be so difficult? And yet it was.

From the moment Joe had announced the engagement, her small family wedding turned into a large church wedding.

"We are family, too," church members insisted.

Even though Kathleen had been attending church for two years and even volunteered, becoming accepted by church members, she was still unsure about what it meant to be a pastor's wife. They had talked about it repeatedly over dinners together, drives, walks, so much that Kathleen figured she knew what she was getting herself into when she said yes, only to question that yes immediately afterwards when Joe announced it to the congregation. There was applause, and then congratulations from all sides. Kathleen wanted to slip away and hide. It wasn't that she disliked the lime-light, she just didn't like "this" lime-light. She had only recently become comfortable in the church, finding a place for herself. Now that had changed. How was she going to fit into her new-found status? Was she really ready to live in a fishbowl?

She didn't want a fuss, didn't want a long white gown and veil, just a simple white dress that she could wear again. But she did want a party.

"Let me take care of everything," said Julia, Kathleen's best friend and maid of honor.

Julia had tried to take over the wedding planning. But Kathleen had responded, "And let you turn it into a fancy southern gala? No way."

"No, that wouldn't be you. Your wedding needs to reflect you and Joe. Trust me."

Joe had wanted to hold the wedding during a Sunday service.

"That may work for you, but not for me," she had told him.

They finally agreed on a Saturday afternoon service with the whole church attending. And then there was the extended family from Joy's Dance Studio and Center for the Arts. And the people from the hospital Joe had come to know through his ministry there. And just about the whole town. Kathleen wore a simple mid-length white dress and white hat, her soft, dark curls flowing to her shoulders. The reception was in the church hall and included a pot-luck dinner put on by church members, with drinks and dancing. Some church members had frowned on the need for drinks at the wedding of their pastor, but those voices had been drowned out by other voices.

"There won't be alcoholic beverages at the reception, will there, Pastor?"

"Why, yes, there will be. Jesus liked a good party. That's why he made sure there was plenty of wine at the wedding in Cana. Who am I to do something different?" Joe had responded to the complaints while Kathleen stood by and smiled.

"Then will the party go on for three days the way wedding parties did in Biblical times?" another asked.

"No, we will part with the Bible on this," Joe told them then took her arm and excused himself.

"You won't be hiding in the bathroom?" Julia asked Kathleen while helping her get ready. Kathleen had been known to slip out of parties or spend extra time in the bathroom.

"It's my party. Why would I?"

"Just checking."

With music provided by a DJ, they could have danced all night. Joe and Kathleen slipped out about ten and headed to their hotel in Detroit. The party broke up by eleven and the hall was cleaned and ready for church the next day. Joe had arranged for a fill-in minister for services that Sunday and the next.

They had said no gifts, but were pleased by the gift of a honeymoon. Their married life had been off to a good start, until that early morning phone call. The first of many phone calls, she figured. That was part of a pastor's life and therefore part of the life of the pastor's wife.

Joe had insisted she attend the gatherings for pastors and their spouses. It used to be for pastors and their wives, but that had changed. The term was no longer an accurate reflection of reality. More women were entering ministry, hence the number of pastors' husbands was approaching the number of pastors' wives. And those husbands were changing the shape of what it meant to be a pastor's spouse. The men weren't expected to be a second, unpaid employee of the church, the way women had in the past. It was understood that most pastors' wives now had jobs, even careers of their own. Still there were expectations that came with the position. She wasn't just marrying the man's family, she was married to the ministry, even if not a minister herself.

"The worst are those phone calls from people in crisis. They always come at the worst possible time, in the middle of the night or during a family celebration."

"That's just part of being a pastor's wife," a more seasoned member of the group had explained. "It's no worse than being married to a corporate executive who's called away on business, or a doctor who is on call."

That may be so, Kathleen thought, but that didn't mean she had to like it.

Chapter 6

Bare walls. Uncomfortable bed. The smell of antiseptic. Now, where was she? Esther scanned the confines of what appeared to be a hospital room. There were a few personal items on the night stand, her comb and brush, body lotion, reading glasses. The last thing she remembered was Kathleen's wedding. Why was Kathleen here? She was supposed to be on her honeymoon. Why won't the words form in her mouth? Someone was speaking but she wasn't making sense. Maybe she could write her question. She saw a tablet of paper and a pencil on the tray in front of her. When she tried to write, the letters came out as a scribble. Her hand would not cooperate.

"It's all right, Esther," Peter's voice. She recognized him. "Kathleen's back from her honeymoon. You're in a rehab facility. You've had a stroke."

A stroke. How could that be? She was the healthy one, eating fruits and vegetables, twigs and berries, as Peter called them. Peter was the one who ate meat and cheese and the occasional vegetable, if she covered it with enough cheese.

"Hi, Mom. How are you today?"

Why are they treating me like an invalid? I've got to get out of here.

"Easy, Esther," Peter stopped her. "Do you want to get up? I'll get someone to help you."

What's he talking about? I can get up on my own. She slid her left leg off the bed. There, now the right. Why wasn't it moving? Peter took hold of her and helped her move her leg.

"I've got this," she wanted to say. Instead she struck at Peter with her left arm, fighting his help. Two nurses came into the room and stood on either side of her.

"Did you want to get up, Mrs. Blake? We'll help you."

Esther stopped fighting. It wasn't worth it. And she was tired. She didn't resist when they lowered her back into bed. That was enough for now. Tired … must sleep.

The first month of recovery was a haze for Esther. She slept almost twenty hours a day as her body slowly repaired the damage done by the stroke. Each time she woke up she had to be told where she was and what had happened. She didn't remember anything beyond the wedding. The wedding was a good memory. It had been embedded in her brain by emotion. Every time she saw Kathleen she wondered, what she was doing there, wasn't she on her honeymoon?

"It's okay, Mom," Kathleen told her repeatedly. "I'm back from the honeymoon. You didn't cause me to miss it. I'm home now. You've had a stroke." And then Esther would struggle to get out of bed or to write what she wanted to say. She was learning to write with her left hand, but even then the words didn't always come to her. But this was okay because she didn't remember. And since she didn't remember, she didn't worry. It wasn't like her to not worry, but she didn't worry about that either.

As she got better at writing with her left hand, she wrote notes to herself to help her remember so people who visited didn't have to keep repeating the same things.

"Stroke," she wrote down. She wrote the day of the stroke and the day's date to help her reference how long it had been. But then the numbers didn't always make sense.

Kathleen came every day and filled the time with small talk. She told Esther what was happening at Joy's Center for the Arts and at church. It didn't matter when she repeated herself because Esther didn't remember anyway, or if she remembered, she couldn't say so. The words all ran together in her head. Esther knew it was just a way for Kathleen to fill up the time. Small talk. She longed to tell Kathleen to stop repeating what she already knew. Instead, Esther would throw her spoon in frustration. When her hand refused to cooperate and write the words she wanted to say, she would throw the pen. When Kathleen tried to help her, it made her angrier. Then Kathleen would leave. But Kathleen always came back.

Some days, Esther would wake up and see Grace, her ten-year-old granddaughter, sitting by her side reading.

"Hi, Grandma. It's me, Grace," she would say then sit in quiet with her. The rules about visitors were laxer in rehab than the hospital. Esther liked this better than Kathleen's chatter. It took too much effort to listen, try to remember, try to talk. It was nice to have company.

And every day, Peter came, only sometimes she didn't remember who he was. Where was Dale? Dale was her husband. Who was this man? He seemed nice, but who was he?

"It's me, Peter."

"Nice to meet you. Do I know you?" she wanted to ask, but her mouth couldn't form the words. "Who?" she managed to get out.

"Peter, your husband." Peter wasn't my husband, Dale was. Where's Dale?

"No, Dale," Esther formed the words.

"Dale's at work," Peter answered. What did he mean, Dale's at work? Why isn't he here with her? Wait, didn't he die, years ago? Did he mean her son, Dale Jr? Not her husband? So confusing.

Some days Peter sat, read the paper, didn't say anything. Who is that nice man, she wondered? She wrote his name on her tablet. She would try to remember him.

Grace liked visiting her grandma at the rehab facility. She was able to come and go as she pleased. When her dad or stepmom weren't able to take her, she would hop on her bike and ride over.

She sat quietly in her grandma's room and read while Grandma slept or she visited other residents of the facility. She knew them and they knew her. She made sure to stand on Mr. Potter's right side when she stopped to say hello. He couldn't see anything on his left side. When she first saw him and said hi, he had appeared shocked even though she had been in plain sight, standing next to him on the left side of his chair. She learned from her mistake and now was careful to stand on his right side before speaking so as not to startle him again.

She sat with Mrs. Humphrey, a young woman who had had a stroke after giving birth to her first child. She would cry when her husband came to visit with the baby and she struggled to hold the child with her good arm. Grace would get her ice cream from the refrigerator in the staff room after those visits. Sally, Mrs. Humphrey, loved ice cream. Grace would sit while Sally ate ice cream on a stick. Grace caught any stray pieces of the chocolate that coated the ice cream and wiped Sally's face for her afterwards.

"Here," Sally motioned to Grace to come closer and pointed at a bag attached to her wheelchair. Inside were pictures of Sally's baby and pictures of her before the baby was born.

"She's beautiful," Grace said as she examined at the pictures. "Just like her mother." Sally smiled. Grace wiped away the tear that slid down Sally's face.

Not all of the residents of the facility were stroke survivors. Grace just liked them better. There were a number of people Grandpop's age. They doted on her, giving her candy and peppermints from their stash. Grace hesitated before accepting the candy.

"Go ahead, honey. It's all right," A nurse standing close by told her.

After the okay by the nurse, she never turned down a sweet, despite being teased mercilessly by her brother about her size.

"Roly-poly, Grace. Gracie, Gracie, two by four, can't get through the bathroom door," Jacob would taunt her then call her graceless.

"It's just baby fat," her grandma had assured her. "You'll lose it once you hit a growth spurt." Grandma always used to know the right thing to say.

In turn, Grace would do things for the residents, get items out of drawers for them, open doors so they could maneuver the hallway, and get drinks from the staff breakroom.

"Keep this up, and we'll have to start paying you a salary," one of the nurse assistants told her. "You better not be taking my job," she teased.

"She's an old soul," Grace remembered hearing her grandma tell her dad. She wasn't sure what Grandma had meant by it, but she liked it. If her grandmother had said it, it had to be good. Her grandmother never said anything unkind about anyone.

Sometimes she brought Lucky with her, when her dad or stepmom had time to drive them both there. The residents liked seeing Lucky.

"No Lucky today?"

"No, Mr. Evans. I rode my bike."

"Give him this from me," he pressed a milk bone into Grace's hand. Lucky fit in with the rehab patients. He had been Ashley's dog for years but ever since Ashley joined that band of hers, that was all she did, all she talked about. She didn't have time for Lucky. But that was okay. Grace didn't mind. She liked taking care of Lucky.

He had become a part of the family eight years ago, before her mom had died. Grace had only been a toddler then. She didn't remember her mom. What memories she did have, she didn't know whether they were real or made-up. She had memories of a woman with a wan face hugging her and laughing with her and then she had been sad. Had that really happened? Real or not, she clung to those memories. They were all she had of her mother.

"How old is he?" one of the patients asked.

"He's fourteen years old."

"That's pretty old in dog years." Grace realized this. Lucky didn't run the way he used to. The vet said he had arthritis and told them to give him aspirin for pain. He was gentle with the patients, laying down next to them, letting them pet him. Ashley didn't even notice how old Lucky was, but Grace knew.

Lucky wasn't able to climb the ladder into the attic where Ashley had taken up residence. It had bothered Grace at first, Ashley abandoning her to have her own room, but she got over it and liked the fact that Lucky stayed with her most nights. He still made his rounds of the house, stopping at Jacob's room for his evening ear rub. But he always ended up in her bedroom for the night.

Upstairs, Grace would hear Ashley playing her guitar and singing to herself while Grace hugged Lucky and let him sleep on her bed. He had become her dog.

Grace finished her rounds, said hi to the birds at the end of one hallway and made faces at the fish in the lobby before returning to her grandmother's room.

"Hi, Grandma."

"Gracie, you still here?" she struggled to say.

"I like it here." Her grandmother was doing so much better. She still had to search for words and sometimes used the wrong word, but Grace understood her. Grandma was learning how to walk again and using her left hand to replace the right one she had depended on for so long but which refused to do her bidding.

"Go outside, play. Don't stay here. We're old people."

"Sally isn't old."

"You know ..." Grandmother wasn't able to complete the phrase

"Yes, Grandma, I know," Grace knew what her grandmother meant. That didn't mean she agreed with her.

"Go on. Get out," Grandma shewed her away.

That was okay. Grace knew she would come back.

Chapter 7

Time has become unstuck. Esther scrutinized the familiar surroundings. Her couch, soft and cushy and perfectly formed to her body after all these years. Her dad's lift chair. The cream-colored curtains. The TV. The stairs. It smelled like home. A slight whisper of lilac remained in the bathroom.

She wondered, where am I in time? Will Dale come downstairs to greet me, taking the stairs two at a time? Who was that woman? It couldn't be Kathleen, not her little girl. The scent of eggs and bacon sifted in from the kitchen. She shook her head. Peter and her dad, left on their own. It helped anchor her in time. They needed her.

"Where ...?" she struggled to say.

"Mom, you're home," Kathleen answered.

Esther shook her head. The house was familiar, but when was it? She struggled to find the words.

"When ...?"

"It's Tuesday, Mom."

Esther shook her head again. Peter touched her shoulder, "You're home, dear."

Who was that man? Oh, yes, Peter. Then this must be, what year was it? They used to post the day, month and year at that other place. What was that place? A prison? A prison for old folks. But she wasn't old, was she? How old was she? Ether grasped the bars of her walker and stared about the room, trying to figure out the answer to her questions, questions she couldn't ask. The words wouldn't come out.

She slipped back and forth in time. Sometimes she was a little girl, riding her tricycle. And then she was newly married with a little girl of her own riding her old tricycle. She hated to be jerked out of the memories to the present. The past was so much sweeter. Why couldn't she live there?

Esther remembered a little girl, four years old, riding a red trike, a Radio Flyer, up and down the sidewalk in front of her house as her mom sat on her swing on the front porch and watched. The little girl waved excitedly each time she rode by, headed off in one direction to the end of the sidewalk, waiting for her mother to call her back. Then she rode back in the other direction. This time, though, Mama didn't call her back. Esther stopped and looked back at her house. Why didn't Mama call to her? She turned her bike around in order to see what was happening. There was Mama, leaning against the porch railing, bent over and crying. Why wasn't Mama looking at her? What was wrong? She didn't know what to do.

"Essie," Mama looked up and called. "Essie, come home." Mama put her hand around her large belly, cradling it as she called. Esther didn't want to go home. Something was wrong. It must be something terrible. She didn't like seeing her mama like this. "Essie, hurry up."

A neighbor came out and called to Mama, "Carolyn, are you all right?"

"No," Mama said. "Would you get Esther? I think the baby's coming."

Mrs. Jordan hurried down her steps and took Esther by the hand. "Do you want some cookies?" Esther liked Mrs. Jordan's cookies. Mrs. Jordan invited her and her mother over for cookies every time she baked a new batch. Esther shook her head yes and climbed off of her tricycle, one hand holding onto Mrs. Jordan.

"What about Mama? I want Mama." Esther stopped.

"You can't have Mama right now." Esther's thumb slipped into its accustomed spot in her mouth. Esther was no stranger to Mrs. Jordan's kitchen and her big sugar cookies. She was torn between wanting their sugary goodness and wanting her mama. The sugary goodness prevailed as she walked into Mrs. Jordan's kitchen and let her lift her into a seat at the table.

"Your mother is going to have a baby. You're going to be a big sister," Mrs. Jordan told her.

"I'm Mama's baby."

"That you are. You will always be your mama's baby, but now your mama will have another baby."

Esther heard a knock on the door and a familiar voice.

"Daddy!" she exclaimed from her height in the chair. "Where's Mama?"

Her father gave her a quick hug and glanced over her head to Mrs. Jordan. "I'm taking Carolyn to the hospital. Can you watch Esther until her grandmother gets here?"

"Of course. I'm happy to. Esther and I are good friends, aren't we, Esther?"

"Where's Mama?" Esther continued to ask.

Her father squatted down in front of her and stared directly into her face. "Your mama is going to the hospital. When she comes home, you'll have a baby brother or sister. Remember, we talked about this. Now you have to be strong and stay with Mrs. Jordan until Grandma gets here. Can you do that for me?"

Esther didn't want to stay there, and she didn't want a baby brother or sister. She wanted her mama. But she didn't want to disappoint Daddy either. She glanced away from him.

"Can you do that for me?" her father asked again, raising her chin so she couldn't avoid looking at him.

"'Kay," Esther said, slipping her thumb back into her mouth.

"That's my girl." Her father gave her another hug. "Her grandmother is on her way. It shouldn't be too long," he told Mrs. Jordan as he stood up.

"Don't you worry. Esther and I will be just fine, won't we Esther?" Esther refused to answer. She sucked her thumb until her father left and Mrs. Jordan coaxed her with another cookie.

Esther loved it at her grandmother's. She got to sleep in a ginormous fluffy bed, big enough for ten people, or so she thought. She slept in the middle with pillows on either side to keep her from falling out. Grandma smelt of liniment and lilacs. She poured liniment on her aching knees and feet each day. Esther would watch her from her perch at the table. Then she would wash with lilac soap. Grandma loved lilacs. Each June she cut sprays of lilacs from the trees around her house, filling her home with their scent. The rest of the year, when she couldn't have the real thing, she used lilac scented air fresheners and perfumes.

Daddy had said it would only be a few days. But Mama was gone for forever, two whole weeks. Even though she liked it at Grandma's, she felt like she had been banished from her home. Daddy said there was something wrong. Mama had to stay at the hospital and get better. When Daddy took her to see Mama, Mama didn't get out of bed. Mama hardly noticed her. Esther sucked harder on her thumb.

Then Daddy showed her a baby. "This is your baby brother, Robert." Esther pulled her thumb out of her mouth.

"Do you want to hold him?" Esther shook her head, yes. She crawled up into the chair in Mama's hospital room, her eyes wide as she waited for Daddy to lower Bobby into her arms. Daddy kept close watch as she held him. He smelt of baby powder and oil and newness. Like the baby shampoo Mama used to wash her hair. Then Daddy took him away and she had to go back to Grandma's.

Esther remembered her mother had not been herself for some time after that. She didn't know why. She just knew that her mother was sad and didn't always take care of Bobby when he cried. Sometimes she would take a bottle out of the refrigerator and feed Bobby herself.

Her grandmother said her mother needed to stop fussing about what couldn't be and focus on what she had. Esther hadn't understood what her grandmother meant.

Her mother had always wanted a large family. But after Bobby, she didn't have any more children. Esther didn't know why.

"Wake up, Carolyn," Esther remembered her grandmother telling her mother. "Look at those two youngsters. They need you. You have to go on for them. You have to be strong for them."

Esther remembered because her mother had said the same thing to her after Dale's death.

Peter helped her to the large electronic chair in the front room. But that was her dad's chair. Where would he sit? Peter raised the chair up to an almost standing position so she could lean back into it and feel the leather against her before letting go and sliding into the seat as Peter worked the controls to lower her to a seated position. He slipped off her shoes and put on her favorite furry, brown slippers, the ones she wore when she was done for the day and wanted to put her feet up.

"These will keep your feet warm and be more comfortable than shoes," Peter said as he slipped them onto her feet.

"You can watch all your favorite movies and TV shows," he said as he turned on the TV. "Look, we've got Turner Movie Classics and Lifetime." Esther cried as she remembered their disagreements about what to watch. Is this what she had become? That woman who watches Lifetime movies and old musicals in her slippers? Peter gave her the remote so she could change channels. Her fingers didn't do what she commanded them to do. She threw the remote.

Peter picked it up and changed channels for her. She was too tired to disagree as Gene Kelly appeared on the screen, dancing with what appeared to be a rain thingy … what do you call it? Something to keep the rain off your head. Why couldn't she remember the word?

Peter joined Kathleen in the kitchen where she had slipped away to fix her mom some lunch. Even she couldn't spoil a sandwich, pb & j. Something Esther could hold.

"She's watching TV."

"Are you sure you can handle this?" Kathleen asked while spreading peanut butter. "Because I know I can't."

"She'll do better in familiar surroundings." Peter had insisted on bringing Esther home once she was able to move around on her own. "She can sleep downstairs until she's strong enough to ride the chair lift." Esther could walk with a walker and feed herself, mostly. She struggled to use her left hand, while regaining dexterity in her right hand. She could speak, but only with great effort — effort that left her tired out and groggy. Still she had shown improvement during the month she had spent in rehab. Peter was going to help her with her exercises. A physical therapist was coming three times a week to help out and a nurse would come once a week, more if needed.

"Besides, your grandpop and I were going crazy in this home alone. We're tired of batching it." Peter could tell he wasn't fooling Kathleen. Still, the fun of being a bachelor wore off quickly.

"Looks like we are batching it for a while," Peter had said to Erick, Esther's father, after Esther was moved to rehab. Erick had been living with Esther since his wife had died more than twenty years ago.

"Could be worse," Erik had responded.

"Yes, at least we don't have to eat Kathleen's cooking." Both had laughed at that.

"I can make a mean meatloaf, old man," Peter had added.

"And I can still fry eggs."

"Hmmm, meatloaf with eggs on top. I think you've got something there." Still, Peter was ready to have Esther home, even if it meant more work for him. "What else do I have to do with my time? Besides, the sooner she gets better, the sooner we can get on with our lives." Peter and Esther had been making plans to travel before this happened. It had been a challenge to get Esther to agree to leave her family for extended vacations, but she had finally gone along with him.

"After the wedding. We'll go after the wedding," she had assured him. Now she had gone on a trip, one into her own head. One without him.

It wasn't how he had imagined his retirement. It was what it was. Tomorrow is another day, as Esther always said. Tomorrow will be a better day, and tomorrow, and tomorrow and tomorrow. Each day would bring her closer to the girl he had married. That was what kept him going.

"You can go home, now," Peter told Kathleen. "I'll take it from here." Peter took the plate with pb & j sandwich cut in quarters and strawberry slices from Kathleen. Kathleen started to protest.

"You can come back tomorrow, or tonight. Whenever you want. You are always welcome, but for now your mother and I have to adjust to a new normal, whatever that is. I'm sure you have other things to do."

"I do need to get to the dance studio." Peter knew Kathleen had taken over doing the books, Esther's job.

"So, go. Your mom isn't going anywhere. She'll be here whenever you want to visit."

Peter put the plate onto a tray and brought it into the front room. He placed the tray onto the adjustable stand he had bought from a medical supply store.

"Esther, Esther, your lunch is ready," he gently touched her arm but she remained asleep. Peter picked up the remote and sat down next to his wife. He sighed as he reached for one of peanut butter and jelly quarters and surfed for something to watch.

Chapter 8

Kathleen hurried off the porch and into her car after saying goodbye to her unresponsive mother. Kathleen fought back tears each time she climbed into her car after visiting. Who was this woman and what had she done to her mother? All these changes. A new home, new life, and now a new mother, one who was a stranger to her. What else would change? She hated seeing her mom like this. She hated the relief she felt when given permission to leave. She hated the guilt she felt about her relief. She was not her mother. She was all too aware of that. Her mother had been the caretaker in the family. She could give and give without resentment. She was happy to give. Kathleen, not so much. She thought she had come to terms with her own selfish nature. God loved her despite her sins. So why couldn't God just leave her be, continue to accept her as she was instead of throwing hurdles across her path to jump over or avoid through going around them?

"Is that what this is? Just a hurdle, a problem for you to deal with, overcome? What about your mom? All she is dealing with?" Most of all, Kathleen hated the voice in her head that continued to challenge her. Some days it sounded way too much like Joe, other days it sounded like her mom.

Her mom … what was she to do without her? This woman, this vacant, unresponsive woman was not her mom. She wanted to shake her, ask her what she had done to her mother, call forth the real Esther Reese-Blake. This woman was not her mother. She would never accept that. There, and if not her mother, she needn't feel guilty about not taking care of her twenty-four seven. Besides, she had issues of her own. She loved Joe, but sometimes she wondered, "Who am I in this relationship? Where am I?" She didn't know how to be a couple. Sometimes she felt as lost as her mother appeared.

Her mom … Where was she now that she needed her? All of her life, even when on the outs with her mother, her mom had still been the one person she could count on. Oh, she didn't always get her way, quite the contrary. They often butted heads, especially in high school. Still her mom was her rock, a stable force in her unstable life. What was she to do without her rock?

"You must become that rock," Kathleen heard that voice again. But how? No answer. Somedays, she hated the voice in her head, hated its demands. Hated its silence. Today was one such day.

Too many changes. Where could she find stable ground?

Kathleen pulled into the parking lot of the Center for the Arts, home of Joy's dance studio. Here was stability. Here was home. Here was her saving grace.

"Aunt Kathleen," Mary, Chloe's little girl ran to greet her as she walked up the stairs to the dance studio. Kathleen picked her up, hugged her and carried her down the hall. The term "aunt" was an honorary title. Chloe had shown up pregnant over four years ago to stay with her grandfather, a supporter of the dance studio. Through him she had started to work there. With her background in dance, she was a natural to take on the running of the studio when Letty, the former director, had left.

"I'm going to add a new dance class," Chloe greeted Kathleen as she walked into the office they shared. "Lyrical Dance."

"Really. What's that?"

"It's like a cross between ballet and jazz. It's more emotive, expressive, than ballet. It tells a story."

"You think there's enough interest to fill a class?"

"Everyone's talking about it. Especially because of those dance shows like, 'So You Think You Can Dance,' and 'Dancing with the Stars.' Don't you watch them?"

"Sure." Kathleen was embarrassed to admit she didn't. Here she was, director of an Arts Center. Her taste in TV viewing tended more towards Breaking Bad and other shows, not reality TV or all of the contests like American Idol and America's Got Talent.

"Then you know about it. It's more free style."

"Not like hip hop or street dance?"

"No, not at all. It's choreographed, usually to a song about freedom or overcoming an obstacle. We can offer this class to our older students. Require that they have two years of ballet before taking it. We have to keep providing more options to our teens or we'll lose them." Kathleen was all too aware of this.

"We can advertise it: As seen on 'So You Think You Can Dance,'" Chloe continued.

"Who will teach it?'

"That's the best part — Letty."

"What? What are you talking about? Letty's in New York." Just hearing Letty's name mentioned was enough to bring a smile to her face.

"I know. She told me she could do a couple weekend intensives, using everything she's learned with Alvin Ailey. Since they'll be on the weekend, the classes won't interfere with our other regularly scheduled classes."

"She'd be willing to fly from New York to do this?" The smile broadened and crept further across her face despite herself. This was too good to be true, she told herself.

"She has to visit her parents some time. She just needs to know her schedule and find a few free weekends. We can offer it over three months in the winter. What do you think?"

"I think so, sure. I love it. Make it happen." Letty had been dancing with Alvin Ailey Dance Troupe for the past two years, after completing her time with Alvin Ailey II. She was a bit of a celebrity at the studio. She visited whenever in town. A hometown girl made it good. She was a symbol to the students of what they could do if they really wanted it. Not that many of them aspired to dance professionally. Still, if they did, Letty showed it was possible. If Letty taught the classes, she knew she could fill them.

No, she didn't have any budding dance stars growing under the studio's tutelage, though some girls did aspire to make it on one of those dance competitions. The closest thing she had to a dance star was Ashley, and Ashley was showing no desire to follow in her mother's footsteps. Kathleen figured that out when Ashley had decided not to compete in Irish step dancing despite making it to the World Championship after only one year of classes. It just wasn't her. She still took ballet classes twice a week, keeping up her "en pointe," but showed no desire to do anything more with it. She was far more interested in her music, though where it would take her, Kathleen didn't know.

Kathleen retreated to her desk and quietly googled lyrical dance. "Have to know what I'm promoting," she told herself as she clicked through websites.

"Lyrical dance is expressive, subtle and dynamic, expressing emotions through movement. It is a combination of intricate, highly technical, and natural moves. Lyrical dance is often choreographed to a song about freedom, of releasing a sad emotion, or of overcoming obstacles, but can be choreographed to any human emotion-related song," she read. She may not have known what lyrical dance was, but she certainly knew about overcoming obstacles. Seems her whole life had been a lyrical dance. She just didn't have a name for it till now.

She went to YouTube to watch some examples.

Chapter 9

"Why do you run so funny?" Grace heard the voice of one of her classmates, taunting the new girl at school. Grace watched the new girl, she thought her name was Josie, try to keep up with the rest of the kids in their game of hide and seek. Her foot raised in a high stepping gait Grace had never seen before. Then her foot dropped and drooped behind her. The girl had been smiling and laughing until the question had been raised. Grace saw the girl stare at her teaser, allowing her shoulder length brown hair to hang forward into her face, not understanding what he was talking about. She stopped running.

"I don't run funny," the girl said.

"Sure do." Brad started to mimic her movements, exaggerating them, waving his arms wildly, as other students laughed.

"What are you talking about, Brad?" Grace came alongside the girl and put her arm around her. "You aren't doing it right. I like the way she runs. I'm going to run just like her." Grace turned to the girl, "Come on. We'll show him." Grace ran alongside of the girl, mimicking her gait and laughing. "It's fun," Grace said as they ran off together, leaving Brad and the rest of the group behind.

"Thank you," the girl said after they stopped.

"Don't worry about Brad. He's mean that way. Everybody knows it. No one pays attention to him," Grace said, then added, "Why *do* you run funny?"

"It's just how I run. I didn't know it was funny." Josie glanced down, again allowing her hair to hide her face.

"That's okay. I like it. You're Josie, aren't you?"

"Yes, I am." She tossed back her hair as she raised her head.

"I'm Grace. Let's be friends," Grace smiled as she linked arms with Josie and together they walked back to their classroom.

Chapter 10

"It's okay, Aunt Kathleen." Kathleen walked into the living room and sat down on the couch next to Joe as she listened to her niece's voice over the phone.

"What's okay, Ashley?"

"We don't have to have our monthly sleep-overs any more. You're married to Pastor Joe and I'm busy with my music."

"Wait a minute. Just because I'm married doesn't mean we have to stop our sleep-overs. You can come and stay with me and Joe. There's plenty of room."

"At the pastor's house? That's okay, Aunt Kathleen, but I'll pass. It might be okay for you and Pastor Joe but …"

"What's wrong with staying with us?"

"It just won't be the same."

"Sure it will. We'll go out to eat then come home and watch videos. That hasn't changed."

"With Pastor Joe?"

"He does live here. And you don't have to call him Pastor Joe anymore. He's your uncle now."

"No, thanks, Aunt Kathleen. He'll always be pastor to me. You have to go on with your life and I have to go on with mine."

"What does that mean?"

"It means, the monthly sleep-overs have been fun, but that's in the past." Kathleen's mouth hung open as she clicked off the phone.

"Something wrong?" Joe asked.

"I think I've just been dumped, by Ashley no less."

"What did she say?"

"She said no more monthly sleep-overs."

"There's probably lots of reasons. She's fifteen now. What teenager wants to hang out with their aunt?"

"With their super-cool aunt? Who wouldn't want to hang out with me?"

"I'm happy to hang out with you, Mrs. Michaels."

"Hmmm. I'm not sure I like that name."

"What would you rather be called?"

"How about the Mrs. Most Reverend Pastor Michaels."

"That could be arranged in some circles." Joe laughed and pulled her close to him on the sofa. Still, Kathleen wasn't happy about the phone conversation. Another change she hadn't foreseen. It hadn't occurred to her that Ashley wouldn't want to stay with her at the manse. What was so wrong with the manse? Okay, she had to admit it. Everything. It was kind of creepy, living in a house owned by the church. It felt like the church owned her as well.

She realized it didn't make sense for Joe to move in with her mom, Peter, Grandfather and Scott. Too crowded. So, what was so wrong with this ready-made, already furnished home? Everything. It just didn't feel like home to her.

"Give it some time," Joe had said. "No place feels like home right away. You have to make a place a home. We have to make it our home." Easy for him to say. He was gone all the time. Church meetings, sermon prep, hospital and home visits, counseling appointments. And now he was part of the psych ward "team" or whatever they called it. Dr. Kremer and other staff had been so pleased with his assistance with Dr. Thompson's wife's case two years ago that they wanted him to take on another case, and then another, and another.

"It's just on a case-by-case basis," Joe explained.

"That's how it starts."

"I don't have to do it," Joe said, backing down, but Kathleen knew how much he had enjoyed being part of the team on Laura Thompson's case. How could she say no?

"No. It's okay. I'm busy too." Just not as busy as you, she added to herself. This gave her way too much time in the manse. Even with helping with her mom's care, she was too much alone in that place. Any amount of time was too much. Not that it wasn't a nice place. The church had seen to that. There were three bedrooms and a bathroom upstairs. Dining room, living room, formal "sitting room," kitchen and bath downstairs and a fully finished basement, complete with pool and ping pong tables for youth group gatherings. The upstairs bathroom and the basement had been added some time in the '40s. The "Michigan" stone basement had been replaced with a finished basement. The sitting room had doubled as meeting space for small groups and the basement had been designed for larger gatherings and the youth group. That had been before they had built a new church, church hall and office space. The frugal original church members had built the manse as an extension of the church. It had once held the church offices and the refinished basement had been the place for church socials. Then the church outgrew the original building and built a new church with a hall and office space. That had been a time of great expansion. They had purchased property south of the church and added a grade school and high school.

The manse couldn't completely shake its early roots. Kathleen could still smell the remnants of too many church potlucks and the stale odor of church coffee permeating the building. Perhaps it was the old furniture. She and Joe had discussed getting new furniture, something more modern and that matched rather than the early American garage sale theme that pervaded every room. The only exceptions had been Joe's daughters' rooms. Stephanie and Michelle had insisted on their own furnishings, ones suited to teenage girls. Joe had been content with the bedroom he had inherited from the former pastor.

They were hesitant to incur additional expenses. Kathleen was also afraid that once it was brought up, it would be referred to the inevitable church committee for discussion and they would end up with a hodgepodge of décor. It wouldn't be the same as picking it out themselves in order to make the manse their home. No, Kathleen was biding her time, trying to decide which battles to fight and which to let go.

"This is a partnership, Kathleen. We can work out these issues together," Joe explained. "We can talk to the church leadership."

"Then how come it feels like war to me?"

"Maybe you are making it one. Give it a chance You saw how supportive the church leaders were of me taking on the extra work at the hospital."

"That's only as long as it doesn't interfere with your work at the church."

"As it should be." Kathleen turned away in frustration. Joe turned her back around and pulled her into a bear hug. "It will work out. We can buy a few things ourselves. What would you like to get first? We can make this a home you can feel comfortable in."

"The first thing to go is this couch," she said. They had been looking for a couch but hadn't found the right one yet. It has to be something suitable for a church manse, Kathleen thought with a sigh.

So many changes. And then there was the change in her relationship with her mom. Peter was the primary caregiver, but there was only so much he could do. He needed her help more than he would admit. Kathleen was sure of that. And he had Grandpop to take care of as well, though Grandpop would fight anyone who suggested he needed being taken care of.

She and Joe had talked about maybe having Grandpop move in with them, at least until her mom was her old self. They had the space, but they didn't have the chair lift on the stairs or a ramp.

"We can ask the church board to make the manse handicap accessible. It's not unreasonable," Joe had suggested.

"And by the time it was done, Grandpop would be gone."

"Not every decision takes forever."

"Really, Joe? Don't you have to run it by several church committees, the finance committee, the building and grounds committee, the board ..."

"Okay, decisions by committee do take a while," he admitted.

"Besides, I doubt Grandpop would be willing to move." Kathleen sighed again. Having Grandpop here would have made it feel more like home. Maybe it wasn't just the furniture. When her boys came to visit, would they want to stay here? Scott had already moved into her old room in the basement. Chances are Josh would want to stay in his own room at Mom's. Who can blame them? Another reason why this place will never feel like home.

Her mother would be her own self before they make this place accessible, or would she? Kathleen had been doing some research on strokes. Some regain almost full use of the affected parts of their body. The brain was malleable. It could take on the work of the damaged, neighboring area. The greatest improvements came during the first three months, but many survivors continue to see improvement years after a stroke. It depended on so many variables, one being the determination of the survivor. Kathleen questioned how determined to get better her mom was. She seemed depressed. Maybe Laura Thompson could help. Laura suffered from chronic clinical depression. She had been hospitalized several times. She was currently in recovery and had taken on the position of church secretary at St. Luke's.

"I don't know," Laura had said when asked. "The depression that occurs after a stroke is different from clinical depression. It's situational."

"How different can it be?"

"Very. She might do better talking to other stroke survivors, but if you think I can help, I'll try."

Kathleen had to admit, what Laura said made sense. "I'll let you know." Maybe there was someone else who could talk to her mom. God knows, she had tried, and failed, miserably.

"I'm just not a good caretaker," she told Joe that night as they laid in bed. "I get so frustrated. I don't know what to do. Mom was always the rock, the mainstay of the family. She took care of everyone else. I don't know what to do with this new person in my mom's body. I could always count on Mom. Now I can't."

"You can count on me," Joe assured her and enfolded his arms around her.

That I can, Kathleen smiled as she relished the feel of his body wrapped around hers.

Chapter 11

At Kathleen's insistence the family was crowded into their kitchen to discuss Esther's care. Peter had gone along with it, picking his battles carefully with his daughter-in-law. This one wasn't worth the effort. Besides, he did need the help, much as he hated to admit. They stood awkwardly about the kitchen. The kids grabbed the seats at the table while the adults leaned against the counter and spoke in hushed tones. Erik sat on his walker.

Ashley was the first to volunteer to skip church and stay with her grandmother, before being asked.

"Hey, how come Ashley gets to skip church?" Jacob whined.

"No one is skipping church. Until your grandmother is able to come back to church, Peter, Ava and I will take turns staying with her," Dale stated.

"No fair," Jacob continued. "I'm old enough to stay with Grandma."

"And that you will," Dale told him. "It's not about being old enough. It's about skipping church. You talk to him," Dale turned towards Ava, trying to assign this argument to her. Ava's gaze clearly said, "Your job, not mine!"

Peter observed the goings on, then intervened. "Look, it won't be that long before your grandma's back in church. I'll take care of her till then. There's no reason for anyone else to inconvenience themselves."

"It's no inconvenience, Peter," Kathleen asserted. "We want to help. That's why we are here. She's our mother and grandmother."

"And she's my wife. You will, and are, helping out. We both appreciate it. But for now, I'll take care of church. Here's when I need the help." Peter put a weekly calendar on the table with time slots marking when he needed help.

Peter finally managed to shoo out the family after setting up a schedule to help him with Esther's care. He had wondered about this meeting, thought maybe it would have been better held somewhere else, but then someone would have had to stay here to take care of Esther. Had she heard the discussion? He hoped she had slept through it.

Esther listened from the living room, straining to hear the conversation taking place, not quite out of earshot, in her kitchen. They must think I'm asleep. Good. More planning and plotting about me and my life without asking me. Like I'm an invalid. Esther wanted to bust into the room and break-up their conversation, only she was having a hard time getting her lift chair to work. The buttons must be on the right-hand side of the chair. What poor planning. Didn't they imagine that someone without the use of their right hand might use this chair? Oh, wait. Wasn't there a remote control? Where was it? Was she sitting on it? Esther sat back in frustration. Maybe she was an invalid.

"What?" Esther asked Peter when her family left and her dad went upstairs for the night.

"Nothing to concern you."

"Were you scheduling babysitters to stay with me? Like I'm a child?"

"No, yes," Peter hesitated. "You do need to have someone with you throughout the day. Your family is just trying to help out."

"I can take care of myself," Esther tried to say but it didn't come out right. Peter understood anyway. Already he was learning her new language.

"I know you believe that, and you will again, someday. But for now, give me the privilege of taking care of you. I want to do this. Who says you are the only one gifted with the ability to serve?" Esther frowned at Peter.

"We were talking about church. Do you think you would be up to going with me this Sunday?"

Again Esther frowned. Peter figured out the answer.

"That's okay, if you aren't ready. Joe will be happy to stop by after church. He can bring you, us, communion."

Esther's frown turned into a grimace.

"What? What's the matter?"

Esther pointed at her Bible. Peter had placed it nearby. Peter handed it to her. Esther shuffled through the pages with her left hand and ended up in the book of Psalms.

"There," she said pointing at a page. "Psalm 31."

Peter glanced at the psalm, unsure what Esther wanted.

"Read it," Esther said.

Peter started to read the psalm out loud. When he reached verse 11, Esther stopped him and indicated she wanted him to read it again. Peter read, "I am the scorn of all my adversaries, a horror to my neighbors, an object of dread to my acquaintances; those who see me in the street flee from me."

Esther nodded her head and told him to continue. "I have passed out of mind like one who is dead. I have become like a broken vessel."

"That's me," Esther put her hand on the page, forcing Peter to stop.

"No, it isn't," Peter put his hand over hers. Esther refused to say more. She shut the book and pushed it away from her.

"No more," she said.

"But you love reading the Bible," Peter said. "You love going to church."

"No more," Esther repeated and pushed the Bible on the floor. How could God do this to her, she thought but didn't have the words or energy to speak. She was a thing of horror. No one wanted to see her, least of all herself.

Bobby was crying. Why didn't Mama get up and feed him? She tried to wake her mother but she just turned away from her. What was wrong? She didn't know how to call Daddy. Mama must be really tired to sleep through Bobby's crying. She went to the refrigerator, pulled out a bottle and shook it the way she remembered Mama doing it. Then she propped the bottle up on a pillow. Bobby drank greedily, the milky white formula sliding out the side of his mouth, his eyes gazing up into Esther's as she reached into the bassinette and held the bottle, climbing on the chair she had pulled over.

Esther didn't remember how many times this happened. At night, she heard her dad get up with her brother, shushing and rocking as he fed him. Sometimes she would get up to see what was happening. "Go back to sleep," her dad would say.

"Is Mama okay?" she would ask around the thumb in her mouth.

"Yes, she's okay. She's just tired. Now go back to sleep."

Esther didn't want to go back to sleep. She wanted to sit up with her father. She wanted him to rock her like he was rocking Bobby, but he shewed her away.

In the morning Daddy would make breakfast and remind her to be a good girl and help her mama. "Mama needs your help," he would tell her. She felt important, being entrusted with such an important assignment.

"Yes, Daddy." Esther took her thumb out of her mouth to reply. But then Daddy was gone and Mama wasn't herself. Esther didn't know what to do.

Esther didn't remember exactly when her mother started acting like her old self. It was as if one day something happened and Mama snapped out of the spell she was under. She started fixing her breakfast again and fussing with her hair. That was how Esther knew Mama was better. Mama always liked to fuss with her hair. She didn't use to like it, used to squirm as Mama told her, "Essie, hold still!" But now she stood quietly in front of Mama as she put spit curls on her forehead and cheeks. Mama was her old self again.

Still Esther continued to take care of Bobby. He was a living, breathing baby doll. Esther felt important. She was needed.

Chapter 12

Julia slipped into the booth across from her, ordered a glass of wine and said, "Tell me. How's married life? Is it amazing?"

This was Kathleen's first chance to get together with Julia since the wedding. Between the honeymoon and visiting her mom in rehab, she had little free time. They had spoken on the phone but that just didn't compare to a tête-à-tête over a glass of wine, or two, or more. Joe had one of his many church meetings tonight so they had agreed to get together.

"Amazing?" Kathleen questioned. What amazed her was how easily the word slipped off of her friend's tongue. If every day-to-day event was "amazing" or "awesome," what word was left for the truly awesome events in life?

"I don't know that I would call life in a manse 'amazing'." Kathleen put up her fingers in quotes for emphasis.

"What's wrong? Isn't life with Joe everything you had imagined?"

"Joe is great, even amazing. It's all the baggage he brings with him." Kathleen loved Joe, loved being married to him. It was his church she wasn't so sure about.

"Everybody brings baggage into a marriage."

"Is that why you and Henry have yet to tie the knot?"

"This is supposed to be about you, not me." Julia put Kathleen off.

"Come on. You know you love to make everything all about you."

Julia laughed. Kathleen's ploy worked. She had managed to get the focus off of her and her relationship with Joe.

"Henry's amazing," Julia said. Kathleen laughed at this, swirled her wine and savored the smell before taking another sip.

"No, he is amazing. I just don't know about marriage. I'm married to my career. He deserves better than that."

Their waitress interrupted their conversation to take their orders. Kathleen glanced over the menu as Julia ordered. Not that she needed to look at the menu. She knew the menu well, still she read it over to see if anything grabbed her attention before ordering her standard, a bacon cheeseburger with a side salad.

"I wish I could get away with eating cheeseburgers and bacon. How I miss bacon." Julia's usual fare was a salad.

"Hey, I ordered a side salad instead of French fries."

"Someday those bacon cheeseburgers will catch up to you."

"Until they do, I'll continue to enjoy them. Maybe I will order those French fries," Kathleen teased her friend. "Can I tempt you with a few fries?"

"Please don't," Julia said.

As they waited for their food, Kathleen's thoughts went back to their conversation. She knew about being married to a career — not hers, but Joe's. She and Joe had discussed this before getting married. She reached for a piece of garlic toast, spread cheese on it and savored the taste as she remembered the discussion.

"I made a mistake, a big mistake, with my first marriage," Joe had told her. "I put the church ahead of my marriage, thinking that was what God wanted. I was wrong. The church and God aren't one and the same. Before I knew it, I had an estranged wife living in the manse with two kids. I promise that won't happen again."

"You bet it won't. The two kids part anyway."

"You don't want kids?" Joe asked.

"Do you?"

"No, but I would if you did. You told me how much you missed out on your sons' lives, all those early years."

"I know, but that was then, this is now. I was a terrible mother back then, abandoning my babies to be raised by my mom. I would probably still be a terrible mother, just in a different way."

"I don't believe that. I think you would be a great mother, if that's what you chose to do."

"I don't choose it," Kathleen insisted.

"Okay. Then I guess it's settled." Joe gave a sigh of relief.

"Was the thought of having kids with me that terrible?" Kathleen reacted to the sigh.

"No, but you know what life with Stephanie was like."

Kathleen was all too aware of how challenging Stephanie had been during her teen years. That was how she had first gotten to know Joe. The meeting had not been a pleasant one since it involved being called to the principal's office where Stephanie and her son, Scott, awaited them. She had blamed Stephanie for getting Scott into trouble, and by extension, blamed Joe. Stephanie had reminded her of herself as a teen, not a compliment. Now, in her twenties, Stephanie was still bringing them together, but not for the best reasons, such as when she was arrested for possession of drugs while in college.

"Still is," Kathleen said. Who knew what else awaited them where this girl was concerned?

"I don't want to go through that again." Joe shook his head at the thought.

"You wouldn't. Every kid is different. And this baby would be different because it would be ours."

"Are you saying you want a baby?" Joe asked.

"No, I just don't want you to be so relieved about it." Kathleen knew she was being irrational, but how can anyone be rational when it came to kids?

Joe's face showed his frustration. "Whatever you say, dear."

"It's complicated. I don't want any more kids and yet I do. Do you understand?"

"Yes," his eyes softened and his lips parted in a smile. "Yes, I get that, and I get you. It's the whole deal, the total package."

"You don't get me. Nobody gets me. I'm my own person."

"I get that as well. Kathleen, why are you making this so difficult? We're on the same side." Joe shook his head and smiled at her. Maybe he did get me, Kathleen thought. She shifted away from that thought and back to Julia.

"Those careers can be a problem," Kathleen said as she finished off the last bite of garlic toast. "But Henry has a career as well."

"But Henry isn't married to his career. He's content as he is, doing what he does. A small town lawyer. No ambition beyond that."

"I thought you liked that in him."

"I did. I do. How did we get on this subject? Anyhoo, I think we're all taking ourselves way too seriously today."

Kathleen laughed. "You had been asking me about married life."

"Let's pick another topic. How's Scott?" Julia took a sip of her wine as she waited for Kathleen's response.

"You tell me. You see him more than I do."

Scott, Kathleen's youngest son, graduated from college a year ago with a degree in business and was now working with her brother Dale in his plumbing business. He was dating Julia's daughter, Alexis. Scott had moved into her room in the basement as soon as she moved out. More private, he had said. What did he need privacy for? She figured it was better than him spending money he didn't have on an apartment.

"Yes, he is at my place quite a bit. Not that I would know since I'm there so rarely."

Kathleen knew. Julia's home was a place to eat and sleep and little more to her. She wasn't sure about all of that unsupervised time Scott was having with Alex at Julia's home. Kathleen knew that Alex living with Julia in Cascades Falls had more to do with Scott than Julia. If not for Scott, Alex probably would be back in North Carolina living with her grandparents. Or she would have stayed in Detroit after graduation or moved to another city. No, the allure of Cascade Falls had nothing to do with her mother, but one young plumber.

"He's spending a lot of time at the business. He's determined to know every aspect of the plumbing business," Kathleen said. Originally Scott had gone to a trade school to become a licensed plumber. He liked working with his hands and had struggled through high school. Kathleen had been surprised when he announced he was going to college for a degree in business.

"Uncle Dale and I talked it over. He said it would be good to have someone with a business degree at the company." Dale was an astute businessman, building his plumbing business from nothing, but he had always regretted not having a degree.

"It's funny how life works out," Kathleen commented.

"How so?"

"Scott, who struggled so hard in high school to keep his grades above a C, was the one who handled college well, while Josh, who breezed through high school on his good looks, charm and athletic ability, struggled with college." Kathleen suspected that had something to do with pretty college girls and parties but chose not to pursue the matter either with Josh or in her mind. Some things are better not known. Josh had struggled to find a major and finally graduated after five and a half years with a major in sports therapy, which he was now using as a physical trainer at a fitness center in his college town. He didn't seem to be going anywhere, had no ambition or goals of which she was aware. Again, she suspected it had something to do with pretty girls and parties. Well, she couldn't say much. She hadn't been any better when his age. She had been worse.

"How is Josh?"

"As far as I know, about the same. I don't hear from him much."

"Alex may be living in the same house with me, but I don't hear much from her either. These kids, they are busy living their own lives. Guess we can't expect much more from them," Julia sighed as she spoke.

"Oh, we can, but we'll be let down."

They had a leisurely meal, continued to get caught up with their lives. Kathleen dragged the time out as long as she could. She didn't want to head back to the manse before Joe's meeting was over, but Julia was ready to get home. They parted about eight. Kathleen called Peter to check on her mom.

52

"She's asleep. Nothing to do here, but you're welcome to come over if you want."

"No, that's okay. I guess I'll head home."

Home. Would it ever truly feel like home to her?

Chapter 13

Peter glanced over at his wife as she woke up with a start from where she was leaning back in her recliner. She shook her head and stared about the room.

"Was I sleeping again?" The words came out slowly, deliberately. She raised her chair to a seated position. He knew he couldn't rush her, knew Esther couldn't trust the words to form glibly on her lips and slide out in correct shape and order. It required concentration on her part to speak. That's why she didn't like visitors, she had told him. They required too much of her limited energy. She needed it if she were ever to get back to her old self, if that was possible.

"You slept through lunch," Peter answered.

"I'm not hungry."

"You have to eat."

"I'm not hungry," Esther restated with emphasis this time.

"You can eat more at dinner," Peter relented. It was a battle, helping her eat, getting her to eat. The first weeks had been difficult. The stroke had affected her ability to swallow. She had to learn to eat without allowing the food to go to her lungs — aspirating, it was called. When the valve that keeps food from going into the lungs and the valve that opens the passage to the stomach are out of whack, this happens. Food does not belong in the lungs. It can cause pneumonia or worse. Esther had already had a bout of pneumonia while at rehab. He didn't want that again. So much to do. So much to learn in order to care for his wife.

It wasn't what he had envisioned five years ago when they had married, but then what did anyone know about what the future held for them? You played the hand you were dealt. That's what he had always believed. Certainly, Esther had done that her whole life, losing her first husband, raising two kids, and then raising her two grandsons. And now this. Life hadn't dealt her the best cards, but she made the most of it. It was the least he could do for her now that she needed him. It was a temporary setback. Soon she would be back to her old self and they could start planning their life again. At least, that was what he hoped for, prayed for.

"No kids?" Esther looked about the room. The whole family made sure someone was always with Esther, that included her grandchildren, Ashley, Jacob and Grace. Especially Grace. Grace was willing to come over whenever asked, even when not asked.

"Good," Esther spoke slowly. "I don't want them here anymore."

"What are you talking about?"

"I don't want them here," Esther repeated. "I don't want them wasting their lives taking care of me." Esther was emphatic as she strained to get the words out.

"They aren't wasting their lives. They like helping out, especially Grace. It's good for them."

"Especially Grace. She needs to be outside with her friends, not inside with me."

"Don't you think they might have some say in this?"

"And you too. I can take care of myself," Esther pulled herself out of her chair and leaned on her walker.

That sounded like the old Esther. She was not one to allow others to take care of her.

"I like taking care of you. Let me do this."

"Well, I don't like being taken care of." Esther started to take a step then sat back down. She pushed her walker over. "I hate that walker." She kicked her slippers off. "And I hate these slippers. I want to wear real shoes. These just remind me how useless I am."

"It's only for a time. You won't need it forever."

"I hate it," Esther repeated. "I hate my life."

"It will get better." Peter didn't like where this conversation was going. This was not what he expected. How could he convince her to keep trying?

"How do you know that?" she asked.

"I just do. Trust me. I promise you, it will get better. You will get better. You just have to keep trying."

"I am trying. I'm tired of trying," she yelled at him then leaned back in her chair. "I don't want to try anymore."

"But you have to," Peter went over to her. "You have to. If not for yourself, then for us, for me. If not for me. Then for your grandchildren," Peter added as he got no response.

"No, I did that once, twice. I kept going after Dale died because of the kids and then there was Kathleen's kids. I can't do it anymore. I'm not going to do it anymore." Esther sunk back, exhausted from the effort. "I can't keep up this charade. I don't know who I am," she mumbled.

Peter looked at his wife. He didn't know who she was either.

Esther watched her four-year-old daughter riding her tricycle up and down the sidewalk as she sat on the steps of their front porch and watched her baby boy toddle around the front yard. How old had she been back then? Twenty-four? Over forty years ago. Why did it seem like yesterday? Oh, yes. She had had a stroke.

Kathleen, ever the spit-fire, would challenge her when she told her to stop. She always wanted to go further than she was allowed, forcing Esther to get up, pick up her youngest and walk after her.

"No more bike," she would tell Kathleen.

"Why?" Kathleen whined.

"You know the rules. If you don't come back when I call, bike riding is over."

"It's not fair," Kathleen pouted as Esther grabbed the bike and rolled it home, Dale Jr. struggling in her other arm. Kathleen refused to budge, crossing her arms in front of her.

Not again, Esther thought as she wheeled the bike home. What am I going to do about that girl? She couldn't wait for her father to get home. At least then she would get some reprieve. Dale had a way with Kathleen. Esther put the tricycle on a safe place in the yard where Dale wouldn't run over it when he came home. As she turned back to get Kathleen, a police car pulled up in front of the house. Esther glanced at her daughter who stubbornly remained where she had left her, then back at the police officer as he got out of the car and approached her.

"Are you Mrs. Dale Reese?"

"Yes, can this wait? Is something wrong? I have to get my daughter." Esther nodded in Kathleen's direction

"I'm afraid there is something wrong. There's been an accident."

"Been what?" she shook her head, not understanding the words.

"An accident."

"My husband, Dale … is something wrong?"

"Yes, ma'am. I'm sorry, Ma'am, but your husband is dead."

"That can't be true. It can't be my Dale. You must be mistaken." What was he saying? Esther knew he had to be wrong. She continued to shake her head, no.

"Does your husband work for the power company?"

"Yes."

"Then I'm sorry, but it's true. Is there someone I can call for you?" Just then Esther saw an electric company car pull up behind the police car. Esther recognized Dale's boss and one of his co-workers. She slid back to the stoop, almost dropping Dale Jr. as she sat down.

"It can't be true," she kept saying. Dale's boss approached.

"I'm so sorry, Esther," he said.

"It was an accident, a terrible accident," Dale's co-worker stated. "I was there. I don't know how it happened. Dale was always so careful about checking everything twice, making sure the power was off. The transformer — it, it blew up."

"It isn't true. It can't be my husband, not my Dale. George," Esther turned to Dale's boss. "Why is he saying this? Why are you letting him say this? Tell him it's not true."

"Esther, it is true. I'm so very sorry."

No, it couldn't be true. Why were they lying to her? Any minute now Dale would drive up with his big smile and wrap her into his arms and plant a kiss on her lips. Any minute now. It couldn't be true. She couldn't accept it. When she tried to accept what they were saying, she couldn't breathe. It was like a crushing weight was on her chest, squashing her heart. She couldn't bear it, couldn't bear the pain. What was that man saying? Why were they lying to her? Make them go away.

"Where is my husband?" Esther struggled to get the words out.

"At the hospital. They did what they could, but they couldn't bring him back. Is there someone, anyone we can call to go with you? Anyone to watch the kids?" Kathleen had appeared at her side. How could she have forgotten her?

"My mother, their grandmother. She'll watch them. My dad will go with me. I'll call them." Esther tried to stand up but slipped back down as her head spun.

"That's all right, Esther. I'll call your parents. I can watch the kids." Her neighbor, Florence, came to her side.

"What do you know?" Esther asked. "Do you know about Dale?"

"I heard it all. Esther, I'm so sorry," she bent down and wrapped Esther in her arms.

"It's not true. I have to go to the hospital to get this straightened out," Esther repeated over and over to herself as she waited for her mom and dad to arrive.

Chapter 14

Esther bumped along the uneven grade of the dirt walkway, pushed by the inexperienced hands of her daughter. They reached the area for picking apples and parked her wheelchair where Esther could see beyond the trees of the orchard and oversee the gathering of the traditional apples for holiday pies. Kathleen breathed in the fresh, crisp autumn air and smiled at her.

"The apple never falls far from the tree," she said, glancing at her mom.

"Except when it does," Esther added.

"What does that mean, Mom. You talking about you and me?"

"No, me." How to make her understand?

Esther had wanted to skip the annual ritual. In previous years, Esther had always supervised the selection of the perfect pie apples.

"Spies," she always insisted. "Spy apples make the best pies."

She would pick them herself and carefully examine the ones her kids and now her grandkids picked. Kathleen had rebelled against the tradition during her youth, continued to rebel once back in Cascade Falls, but had finally fallen under its spell. The crisp air and that first bite of apple newly plucked from a tree — how could anyone resist? Their local orchard allowed kids to munch on an apple of their choosing while their parents filled their baskets. Now Esther wished she hadn't been so insistent on Kathleen joining her each year.

She always made apple pies for Thanksgiving. She peeled and sliced the remaining applies and froze them to be pulled out for Christmas and other special occasions, or just because, during the rest of the winter. Nothing warmed a frozen Michigan winter like apple pie still warm from the oven, her mother had told her many times. It was a tedious job, all of that peeling and slicing. For all of her complaining, Kathleen had been won over. She may not have been a good cook, but at least she could peel and slice an apple and then relish its transformation into pie, under Esther's skillful hands.

Kathleen had insisted on taking her this Saturday.

"Joe is busy preparing his sermon and Peter needs a break," she told her. "Mom and I need some girl time," she told Peter. "Right, Mom?"

"No," the word had hardly formed in her mouth before Kathleen had wheeled her out of the house and down the ramp. "The ground is too uneven for your walker, so we're taking your wheelchair," Kathleen had told her before she could protest. She hated her wheelchair. Far too easy for people, meaning her kids, to force her to go where they wanted her to go. She didn't like this role reversal. When her kids had been little, she would walk slowly, at their pace, but when speed was necessary, she always had the option of picking them up and carrying them or plopping them in a stroller. This felt too much like being plopped into a stroller and made to go places she would rather not go.

"Mom, you and Grandma were like peas in a pod. So much alike. You both lived for your family," unlike me, Kathleen added to herself. She had never wanted to be like her mother, made a point of fighting her every step of her life, every milestone. The last thing she had wanted was to be trapped at home with kids. That's why she had been so quick to pass on that responsibility to her mom. Mom was the one who was good at that stuff. Mom was good at taking care of others. Kathleen was all too aware of her failings in this area of her life. She didn't need to be reminded of it. No, she was not like her mom. She had somehow fallen far from the tree. Perhaps a bird had picked her off and carried her away. Or a hungry squirrel carried her off to a nest in a tree far away.

Kathleen watched as family units of three or four or more walked through the orchard, little kids riding on their dad's strong shoulders, babies in wraps, resting on their mother's chest. Little boys and little girls sliding out of their parents' hands and running for freedom, only to be swooped up by their parents before they ran too far. It was a game. These toddlers just wanted the appearance of independence. Not so her. Even at four, she had been bent on her own will. See where it had gotten her. Her life wasn't bad now, but what a circuitous, dangerous route to take. No, if she had been smart, she would have fallen closer to the tree of home and family.

She tried to imagine herself and Joe as one of those families. No, just didn't work. No amount of trying could make it happen. She just didn't fit the mommy mold.

She watched as one little girl in bib overalls and a jean jacket bent down and picked up an apple.

"No, Ariel. Don't pick an apple from the ground. Let Daddy help," her mother scolded. Her dad swooped in, picked her up and swung her onto his shoulders as she laughed and her blond curls bounced. He helped her pick out the biggest, reddest apple from the branch, then put her down safely on the ground. Kathleen wondered if her dad had ever done this with her. It seemed like something he would have done, from what few memories she had of him. No, she was like her dad. A bit of a dare devil, a rebel. At least, that's what she told herself. If she wasn't like her mom, she must be like her dad. It's the only thing that made sense to her.

The little girl held the apple with both hands, brought it up to her mouth and attempted to take a bite. The apple slipped through her fingers and rolled away. She let out a gasp then commenced to cry.

"It's okay, Ariel. You can get another apple," her mother said.

"I don't want another. I want that apple. It was the bestest."

"But it's dirty, sweetheart."

"Here," her dad picked up the apple and polished it with his t-shirt till it shined. "Five second rule."

"Michael, she can't eat that once it's been on the ground," her mother said.

"It's fine. She'll be fine. A little dirt won't hurt her. It's good, clean dirt. Build up her immune system," the girl's dad insisted.

"If she gets sick …"

"I know. I'll be the one staying up with her."

"That's right," the woman said as he planted a kiss on her lips. She patted the small creature wrapped in a cocoon on her chest. A papoose, Kathleen thought. Something tugged at her chest, something buried inside. She caught herself wishing to be part of the scenario that had unfolded before her till brought back to reality by Grace and Jacob.

"Here, Grandma. Is this enough?" Jacob placed a partially filled basket in front of her mom. Dale and Ava had come in their own car with Grace and Jacob.

"Not half enough," her mom said.

"See, I told you," Grace told Jacob.

"Who put you in charge?" Jacob grabbed Grace's arm and twisted it behind her.

"Stop it! Dad!" Grace yelled for her father. Dale and Ava came over the path with two more baskets of apples. Jacob quickly let go of his sister before being caught. Kathleen could see that Jacob had fooled no one, especially not her brother, but Dale had chosen to let it slide.

"Sometimes you have to let the kids work things out on their own," he had told her before.

"Like you and me?"

"Not a good example," Dale responded. Kathleen had been the one to tease her little brother mercilessly until he was old enough to beat her up. Her mom had allowed it. "Mom always liked you better," Kathleen had complained.

"Well, maybe if you had not been so ornery ..." and so it would go. Childhood fights evolved into adult fights. If she had kids now, she would do it differently. She wouldn't let them pick on each other. She would make them be nicer to each other. Kathleen laughed at herself before the thought even had a chance to take root. She knew enough about kids to know the folly of such thoughts. The only way to keep siblings from fighting was to only have one child.

"Are we done now? I don't see why I have to do this. Ashley didn't have to come," Jacob whined. "Can I go in the corn maze now?"

Dale put the baskets of apples before his mother for her approval. Her mother didn't even smile at the abundance before her. Kathleen saw that Dale took her lack of response as an okay and sent Jacob on his way.

"But take Grace with you," he added before Jacob was out of earshot.

"Do I have to?" Jacob stopped long enough to whine.

"You take Grace or you don't go at all."

"She'll slow me down. None of my friends are stuck baby-sitting their sister," Jacob started to say then thought better of it. "Okay, come on," he told Grace.

Grace ran after her brother, her chubby legs taking two steps to every one of his.

"So, Mom, what do you think?" Dale asked. "This should be enough for plenty of pies.'

Her mom sighed. "Can we go home now?" she asked Kathleen.

"Sure, Mom. Dale and Ava can take the apples home. We can go over to their house tomorrow and work on prepping them." Kathleen could tell by the lack of expression on her mom's face that the thought didn't delight her. Perhaps this had been a mistake. At least it got her mom out into the fresh air.

"You know, Mom, if you don't make the pies, I guess I'll have to." Kathleen had been sure that would get a rise out of her mom, but nothing. What was she to do?

She helped her mom out of the wheelchair and into Joe's Chrysler. Her Escort was okay for her, but not for transporting her mom. Her mom slipped easily into her seat, grabbing the handle on the ceiling of the car with her good hand. She closed her eyes and waited while Kathleen struggled to fold her wheelchair and put it in the trunk.

No, maybe this had been a mistake.

Chapter 15

Coming to the apple orchard was a mistake, Esther thought on the drive home. Too many memories. It reminded her of all she couldn't do. And to have to be pushed in a wheelchair ... Shoot me now, she told herself. She guessed Kathleen meant well, or did she? She never could tell with that girl. Yes, the apple doesn't fall far from the tree, except for when it does, like her and Kathleen, like her and her mom. Esther was silent as she stared out the window and watched the orchard disappear from sight.

It hadn't been like that growing up. As a girl she had wanted nothing more than to be like her mother. Her mother had been so beautiful, with her clip-on pearl earrings and necklaces, her stylish dresses and high heels. She had the most beautiful mother in the neighborhood. Of that she was sure. Even during the hard times, when her mother hadn't been herself, she still wanted to be like her mother. She knew it was just a passing fluke. That woman had not been her mother. And she had been right. Her mother had come back to her, though not quite the same. Had her mother changed, or had it been her? She had never been quite sure. She had wanted to be like her mother and have a big house with fine furniture and room for lots of kids. She had been like her mother, until she wasn't. Esther wasn't sure what had brought about the change. She just knew she wasn't like her mother, not because she hadn't wanted to, but because her mother had pushed her in that direction. It hadn't made sense to her as a child.

She remembered coming to the orchard with Dale and Kathleen when they had been little, like so many of the families there today. Those were painful memories of happy days that ended far too soon. After her husband Dale died, she never wanted to come back there, but her mother had forced her to, much as Kathleen had forced her today.

"You have to go. It's a tradition."

"A tradition I'd rather do without, Mom."

"You will do it for those babies. Pies have to be baked and apples have to picked, and you have to help," her mom had asserted.

"Can't you do it without me? Just this time?"

"I let you off the hook last year, but not this year. You are doing more than picking apples. You are creating memories for your kids."

Esther hadn't wanted to create new memories at that time. She had wanted to hold onto the ones she had, ones with Dale. She didn't want memories that didn't involve him. But her mom had insisted. She didn't know where her mother had gotten the strength. Her mother had always seemed so weak to her. Yet she could muster up a will of iron where her grandchildren were concerned. Maybe that was when she had rolled away from the tree?

"The apple doesn't fall far from the tree." She remembered the phrase had been used in her favorite book, *Anne of Green Gables*.

"Mama, what does 'the apple doesn't fall far from the tree mean'?" she remembered asking her mom as she dutifully peeled apple after apple under her mother's guidance. Her father and brother loved apple pies and she loved them, so she accepted the task, learning from the best. Her mom made the best pies. And when her mother died, she took on that role, carefully whisking the flour, lard and water with a fork until every morsel was moist then gathering the dough into two balls.

"The larger one we'll use for the bottom crust," her mother explained. "Don't work the dough so much Essie. It'll make the dough tough," her mother had instructed her. "You want a nice, flakey pie crust. I can usually tell by the feel whether it's going to be a good crust or not. If it crumbles in my hands and is hard to roll out, that's a good sign. If it rolls out like cookie dough, the crust will probably be tough. The secret of a good pie is in the crust." Her mom had been good at cutting corners, but, once lard was no longer available, she always used Crisco. No generic brand would do.

Esther had watched as her mother lovingly rolled out the crust, carefully laid it in the pie pan, then added the filling. After adding the filling, she laid the top, pinched the two layers of crust together and crimped the edges. She cut slits in the crust to let it breathe, then sprinkled a small amount of sugar on top of the crust – "to help it brown," she explained.

"The secret to a good fruit filling is just the right amount of sugar. You want enough to bring out the natural sweetness of the fruit, but not so much to overpower it. Betty Crocker recipes add too much sugar. I always cut the amount in half or more. Apples are naturally sweet. All you need is a tablespoon or two of sugar." Betty Crocker was her mother's cooking Bible. She had passed her copy on to Esther, along with all of her notations in the margins. Betty Crocker was still Esther's go-to cookbook.

"The apple doesn't fall far from the tree. It means, kids grow up to be like their parents," her mom had explained.

"Oh, I like that." At the time it had seemed like a good thing.

"Oh, Essie, you don't want to be like me. I want so much more for you," her mom had said. At the time she didn't understand what her mom meant. Her mom hadn't let her be like her. When Dale died, she wanted to die too. She wanted to curl up into a ball and never come out again. Isn't that what her mom had done when she was a little girl, after Bobby was born? Hadn't her mom died a little back then? Why couldn't she have a breakdown, sink into depression, let other people care for her children, like her mom had done? But no, she had to be strong. But now was her turn. She wasn't like her mom, until she was.

Chapter 16

"Ava, can Josie stay for dinner?" Grace walked into the kitchen where her stepmother was busy cooking. Grace knew her stepmother would say yes. She always said yes to her. Josie stood behind her as she asked.

"Of course, honey," Ava smiled in response. "We'll just set another place at the table."

"I told you it would be okay," Grace told Josie as they ran out of the room.

Grace and Josie had become bffs – best female friends, best buds. Josie was so much fun. She loved to make things and then made up stories. She would fashion unicorns out of Play-Doh and even make tiaras and necklaces for them to wear. Grace loved her magical stories about unicorn land and fairy princesses. She had never been a princess, but when she was with Josie, she felt like one. It didn't matter that Josie ran funny, or that she walked up on her toes sometimes or fell. That was all because of an evil spell. An ogre or evil magician had cast a spell on Josie. In reality she was a fairy with wings to carry her slight body wherever she wanted. The evil ogre was jealous of Josie and her wings, and forced her to walk; but someday her wings would be restored and she would fly away to her kingdom.

"But not without me," Grace would say when Josie told the story. It was different each time but the ending was always the same, flying away home.

"I'll never leave you. I'll send my favorite unicorn to get you. Then you'll join me in my kingdom and together we will reign." Grace never tired of the story.

"Your friend is clumsy," Jacob would taunt her.

"Is not."

"Is too." Why did Jacob delight in torturing her?

"It's what big brothers do," her grandma had told her. She figured it was true, but still didn't understand it.

"That's just boys. He'll grow out of it someday," Grandma had said.

"Like Dad and Aunt Kathleen?"

"Yes, like your dad and your Aunt Kathleen, though I don't know that they're the best example. They still pick on each other. But they love each other, too." Grace wondered if she would ever love Jacob the way Aunt Kathleen loved her dad. When Jacob made fun of Josie to her face, Grace tried to hit him. Jacob put his hand on her forehead, pushing her back, and let her swing away. Not a single one reached him. Then he would grab her and make her hit herself saying, "Stop hitting yourself, stop hitting yourself." He didn't hit hard. It didn't hurt her, only her ego.

"Brothers are mean," Grace told Josie. "Be glad you don't have one."

"But I would like a brother, and a sister."

"I've got a brother and an older sister. You can have them both." There had been a time when Grace had adored Ashley, had followed her around. But now those days were over. A friend was better than a sister or brother.

Grace liked going over to Josie's house. Her parents were both professors at a local college. Their house was full of books and pictures. The sound of classical music filled the house. But most of all she loved Josie's grandmother. She was plump and round and all soft and squishy when she hugged you. She was a veterinarian, though she no longer practiced. She had rabbits and kept stray dogs and other animals in a shed she had made over into her own space. Josie loved the animals and helping Josie's grandma with them.

Her grandma kept Josie stocked with cookies and cupcakes. As Josie's bff, she shared in those treasures. Josie's grandma limped and wore some type of metal support on her legs. Grace spotted them when her grandmother wore skirts and when her pants slid up when she sat down.

"What are those?" Grace asked once while sitting at the kitchen table and snacking on milk and cookies.

"They are braces, for my legs."

"What are they for?" Grace continued to stare at Josie's grandma's legs. Josie's grandmother lifted her skirt so Grace could see them better.

"They support my legs and help me walk, otherwise I would fall down."

"Like Josie does sometimes. Will she have braces too someday?"

"No, I won't," Josie stated, her eyes became furrowed and dark. "I won't have braces, not ever." She jumped up from the table and prepared to leave.

"We can't always determine our future, sweetie. I hope you never have to have braces, but if you do, you will still be okay," her grandma reassured Josie.

Grace didn't see what the big deal was. She liked Josie's grandma's braces.

Chapter 17

"What are we doing for Thanksgiving this year?" Peter asked.

Kathleen, Peter and Dale were gathered in the kitchen out of earshot of Esther to have a family pow-wow. Kathleen grabbed an apple from the bowl on the kitchen counter and took a bite. "We could have it at my house," she suggested.

"You cooking?" Dale raised his eyebrows and frowned.

"I didn't say that, though Joe's pretty good in the kitchen. Just the house. There's plenty of room and we can get extra chairs and tables from the church."

"I was thinking, maybe Ava and I could host this year. We haven't done it yet. I've still got the extra tables and chairs from when Joy and I used to host Thanksgiving," Dale offered.

"No, we have to have it here. That's what your mother would want. We'll all pitch in," Peter said.

"What would I want?" Esther pushed through the door with her cane. "What are you talking about? Why are you talking about me?" Almost five months since her stroke, Esther was getting around with a cane. She had yet to recover full use of her right arm, might never recover full use, but was able to use her left hand for most everything she once used her right hand for. Peter was happy for every bit of progress.

"Ambidextrous, that's me," Esther told everyone who asked. She was still tired and couldn't make it through the day without a nap or two. Words still eluded her at times, especially names, but then wasn't that just part of the aging process, or so Peter reassured himself.

"We were talking about Thanksgiving," Peter said.

"We'll have it here," Esther stated.

"That's what I said," Peter told her.

"Are you sure you are up to it, Mom? Joe and I could host. Or Dale and Ava," Kathleen quickly added when she saw the expression on her mom's face at the possibility of her and Joe hosting Thanksgiving.

"It'll be here. I can still give orders. You all will help out." That was settled. Peter was relieved. More baby steps.

Esther remembered when Dale had surprised her with this house, carrying her over the threshold. She had been eight months pregnant with Kathleen at the time. Still Dale had insisted on carrying her.

"What do you think? Don't you love it?" Esther hadn't been sure. They had been living with her parents while saving money to buy a home. Esther wanted out of her parents' house as much as Dale, still it was such a big step, especially with a baby so close to being here.

"Are you sure we can afford it?"

"I've got the okay from the bank. All I need is for you to say yes. Then it's as good as ours." Dale had been working hard for this day. Esther knew that. He had started work for the electric company right out of high school. He was going to school at night to become an electrical engineer. Eventually he would no longer have to work on the wires, climbing poles, work that scared her. He was determined to provide well for his family. They had married after she graduated from high school. It was all she had wanted, to be married, have a family. Dale was all she wanted. How could she say no to him?

"Say yes, Essie," only Dale and her mom called her that. Coming from her mom, it brought flushes of embarrassment. Her mom was reminding her that she was still her baby. But coming from Dale, it was an endearment. Funny how Dale could redeem all the hurting places inside her, turn them inside out and make them a strength.

She remembered how they had met. Summer tennis camp at the park. They had been playing mixed doubles, on opposite teams. He was new to Cascades Falls, having moved in with his grandparents when his dad had been transferred out of the country by his company. She hadn't noticed him in the heat of the match, so intent had she been on winning. They had been evenly matched, were tied at one game each. Game point. Dale lobbed an easy shot her way. She had been so surprised, she almost missed it. She had expected another hard and fast serve hitting the farthest corner of the in-zone. She had smashed it back at him — point, game match.

Dale's partner had glared at him. He ignored her as he jumped the net, shook hands with her partner and then approached her.

"Good game. That was a great last hit." He grabbed her hand and squeezed it.

"You threw the game," Esther responded.

"Now, how can you say that?"

"Because you did. I didn't want to win that way. Your last serve was a joke."

"Well, then, let me make it up to you. How about an ice cream float?" Dale had not let go of her hand yet. "Come on," he coaxed.

Esther looked down at her hand, caught in a strong grip. "Are you going to let go of my hand?"

"Not till you say yes."

Esther gazed into his blue eyes and sincere smile. Blond curls framed his face. How could she say no?

"I can't. I have to get home."

"Then let me drive you home."

"I've got my bike."

"I'll fit it in the trunk. Come on, you owe me."

"I don't owe you anything, but all right," Esther agreed.

"Great. I'm Dale," he said as he let go of her hand.

"I'm Esther." Esther hated her name, hated having to tell others her name. Could Mom have picked a worse name? No one at school had such an antiquated name. She knew Dale would laugh at her name and abandon her like the other boys at school who made fun of her name.

"Like Queen Esther," Dale stated.

"Queen Esther?"

"Yes, from the Bible. Don't you know the story?"

"I don't know the Bible."

"She was the most beautiful woman in the land. She was chosen to be queen because of her beauty. She saved her people."

"Really?"

"Don't you go to church?"

More reason to be embarrassed. Her parents used to go to church, one time. But then they stopped. Esther didn't know why, or what happened. Sometimes she would attend morning Bible study, more for the donuts than the Bible. She had friends who invited her to youth group activities. Sometimes she went. Others she didn't. She didn't feel any lack in her life until now, now she had to admit her failing to this blue-eyed boy. He didn't seem to mind.

"I'll read it to you some day."

Only he could make her feel good about her name.

Years later, she asked her mom why she had named her Esther.

"For your great aunt Esther. You don't remember her, do you? You were so little when she died. She was my mother's sister and a suffragette. I liked her spirit, admired her strength. So unlike me. She never had any kids. I don't know why. She was married. So I told her I would name my first daughter after her. I wanted you to be strong, like her. And you are strong." Her mom sighed as she spoke. "Back then, I was going to have so many kids."

"What happened?"

"Life doesn't always turn out how you expect it."

"I know. I was going to have so many kids too," Esther said.

Chapter 18

Grace was surprised to see Josie's mom when she and her dad took Lucky in for his check-up.

"I thought you were a teacher," she stated.

"I am, a teacher of veterinary medicine," she said. "I only teach part-time, as an adjunct. I couldn't stand to be in the classroom and away from my animals," she continued as she scratched Lucky's ears and ran her hands over his body.

"Have there been any problems? Concerns? Lumps?" she asked as she continued her search.

"He's slowed down considerably this year," Dale said.

"That's to be expected at his age. Does he seem to be in any pain?"

Her dad glanced at her before answering, "Yes, some days."

"Arthritis. You can give him aspirin to help with the pain. Other than that, he's in good shape for his age. No lumps, no cancer."

"Just old age."

"I'm afraid there's no cure for that," she said as she stood up. "Are you coming over tonight?" she asked Grace.

"Yes." Grace and Josie were having a sleep-over, though she was wondering about going. How could she leave Lucky?

"Josie's looking forward to it." Josie's parents were going away for the night, something to do with the college. Josie's grandmother was watching Josie. She had told Josie she could have a friend over. Grace had been looking forward to it too.

"Can I bring Lucky?" Grace asked.

"Grace," her dad intervened. "Don't you think Lucky will be happier at his own home?"

"Not without me."

"Lucky is welcome too, Grace, if he wants to come."

"It won't be too much on your mother?" her dad asked.

"No, she loves animals too."

"She's a vet, Dad. She'll help me take care of Lucky." How could her dad not know? Grace thought everyone knew Josie's grandmother. "Please," she said, stretching the word out until she received the response she wanted from her dad.

"Okay." She knew Dad would say yes.

"Then it's set," Josie's mom said. "I'll tell Grandma to expect an additional guest." Grace couldn't wait. She walked Lucky back to the car and sat in back with him rather than in the front with her dad.

Ava dropped Grace and Lucky off later that afternoon. Josie was waiting for them.

"Come on," Josie said, taking Grace's hand. She started to run towards the backyard in a lop-sided gate. Josie only ran when with Grace, or so Grace had told her. Grace stopped as Lucky lagged behind.

"We have to wait for Lucky," Grace said.

"Lucky will be just fine with me," Josie's grandmother assured her. "You two run along." She sent them on their way. "It does good to see those two running." She added. "It's good to see Josie doing as much as she can. She will need these memories to hold on to," she told Ava.

"Are you sure they won't be too much for you?" Ava said, glancing at her braces.

"Grace is a joy to have around. And Lucky will keep me company inside while they run around. Won't you Lucky?" She reached down and patted Lucky's head.

"Does Josie … is there something wrong?" Ava had wondered for some time but had not found the opportune time to inquire, until now.

"No, why do you ask?"

"The way she runs. And she comes to the dance studio with Grace but refuses to dance. We, or I, just wondered."

"It's perfectly normal for someone with CMT."

"CMT?" Ava shook her head at the acronym.

"Charcot-Marie-Tooth Disease."

"Is that what you have?" Again, she glanced at her braces.

"Yes, and her father."

"So, it's definite?" Ava wondered how much Grace knew.

"Not yet. Why put her through those tests until necessary, but it does run in the family."

"I'm so sorry." Ava had seen the family at church and wondered. Now she knew. It didn't make it better.

"Why? She's a bright, talented and delightful girl. We are blessed to have her."

"And I see that she is blessed to have you, too." Ava wondered, how could she be so positive? She didn't think she would be if put in the same position.

"God gives us each according to our ability," Josie's grandmother smiled as if she knew what Ava had been thinking. "Would you like to come in for some coffee and homemade cookies?"

"Now I see why Grace loves you so much," Ava smiled. "No, I've got to get home. Let me know if Lucky is a problem. I can come and get him."

"No problem at all." Josie's grandmother waved goodbye as Lucky slowly climbed the stairs into the house. Ava watched Lucky's slow progress. Lucky was in good hands, as was Grace, she assured herself before leaving.

"Why don't you dance with me?" Grace asked Josie as she jumped up from under the tree along the meadow. "Come on. It's fun."

"You know why. I can't dance. I'm too clumsy. I'll fall."

"But there's no one here but me. I won't laugh at you." Grace raised her hands above her head in a clumsy pirouette. "You see, you can't be worse than me. I know I'm no good at dancing, not like Ashley, but I dance anyway. It's fun. You don't have to be perfect to dance. You just have to have fun. I'll teach you. This is first position."

Josie tried to force her feet into the position. They simply didn't work. "I'm sorry, Grace. My feet don't go that way."

"That's okay. We can just free style. Move any way you want."

Josie moved her feet, much like when she ran.

"Move your arms," Grace grabbed Josie's hands into hers and pulled Josie side to side. Josie stumbled and fell.

"I told you I can't do it. If you were my friend, you wouldn't make me," Josie snapped at her as she pulled herself back up.

"I'm sorry, Josie. I just didn't want you to miss out on the fun of dancing even if you are no good at it, like me." Why couldn't Josie see that, Grace wondered?

"Well, I don't want to dance," Josie snapped again.

"I said I'm sorry. Can we still be friends?"

"Okay," Josie shook her head and pursed her lips. "But don't make me dance again."

"I won't. I promise. Does that mean you don't want to go to the Dance studio with me after school anymore?"

"No, that's fun." Josie peered toward the setting sun. "We probably better get back home. Grandma will be waiting for us." They walked back, rather than running. Josie seemed tired, Grace thought, as if the effort to run and dance had taken all of her strength. They walked slowly, side by side, no longer holding hands and laughing. Josie limped a little from her fall, just like Lucky, Grace thought.

Chapter 19

Esther had been in her glory on Thanksgiving, or so Peter thought. She barked out orders, telling people what to do. He almost thought he saw the old Esther, the pre-stroke Esther, return if but for a moment. But only a moment. He could tell how hard it was for her to sit on the sidelines and give orders rather than be in the thick of it. He could see how she struggled to remember what needed to be done, despite the painstaking instructions she had written out for herself weeks before. Her family covered up for her, doing instinctively what they had done in the past with little need for instruction. They covered up so well, he could almost believe his life was back to normal, but it wasn't.

He saw how tired Esther was sitting at the table with all of her family and extended family. She had hardly eaten a thing. He hadn't wanted to embarrass her by encouraging her to eat when he knew she didn't want to. Not in front of her family. He could coax her into eating another time, later, when everyone left.

He had managed to get her to go upstairs to take a nap before dinner. That had been another clue as to just how tired she was. She had never agreed to a nap before this, no matter how tired she was. Not at previous Thanksgivings, not at Kathleen's wedding when he had encouraged her to sit back and relax for a moment.

"I'll relax when I'm old and retired," she had told him then.

She had struggled to smile and greet each new arrival. Even Sara and Larry's twins only brought a faint smile to her face. But there was that moment when the table was set and Joe said the blessing and she surveyed her subjects, her family, that she appeared to him to be the queen she had always been in his eyes. How he had loved her in that moment. If only he could get her back.

Esther had been happy to sit on the back porch after dinner, nodding off as others cleaned up and the kids played in the back yard.

"Another great Thanksgiving dinner," Joe said as he joined her, having been relieved of dish duty for a while.

"No thanks to me," Esther commented.

"What are you talking about? You are the one who brought all of us together. You are the master planner, the conductor who orchestrated the day."

"You can say all you want, but I know it's not so." The more tired Esther was, the harder it was for her to think and speak clearly.

"You know, you have a lot in common with your name sake." Was Joe shifting into pastoral mode, she wondered?

"Who's that?" Esther closed her eyes. It took too much effort to keep them open.

"Queen Esther."

Even in her tired state, Esther had to laugh at that. "Ha, funny Pastor."

"No, I mean it."

"I'm no queen, never been even close to being a queen." Only her Dale had ever called her a queen.

"Esther didn't exactly sign-up to be a queen either. She was conscripted." Joe paused as if waiting to make sure she was still listening.

"Go on," Esther said with her eyes closed.

"You might say she was a beauty contest winner, only she wasn't a willing participant. She was forced to participate. Some might have envied Esther her beauty, but it was also a curse because it drew attention to her. She made the best of her situation and was able to save her people through her beauty."

"I still don't get it, Pastor. I'm no beauty queen."

"No, but you have been put into situations not of your own making or choosing, repeatedly, and did the best that you could with all the grace that you could. In that you acted like a queen. You raised your kids after your husband's death —"

"They were my saving grace," Esther interrupted.

"— And then you raised Kathleen's sons when she wasn't able to. I doubt that was what you had planned for your life, yet you did it anyway."

"How could I not?" Esther stated quietly, her eyes still shut.

"And now you've suffered a stroke. Not something you wanted or planned for, but you are handling it with grace."

"Am I? You think so?" She opened her eyes.

"Yes, good can come out of even this."

"Are you speaking as my pastor or my son-in-law?"

"Both, I guess. Why do you ask?"

"Then as my pastor, I thank you, but what I'm normally too polite to say is, I'll ignore what you said. As a son-in-law, you can shut your trap. Just because you married my daughter doesn't give you the right to tell me how happy I should be about my lot in life." If Esther hadn't been so tired, and if it didn't take so much effort to talk, there was more she would have said. She could tell by the expression on Joe's face that he had gotten her message.

Peter and Kathleen came out on the porch in time to catch the last statement. Esther figured Joe had been taken off balance by the words. Good. Let him try to recover his pastoral dignity. She didn't care.

"What was that all about?" Peter asked. Esther saw that he had been surprised by her rude words, knew it wasn't like her. Too bad. Kathleen shot her a surprised glance as well. Then Kathleen glanced at Joe to see if he was all right. Joe shrugged his shoulders slightly and gave Kathleen a crooked smile. He should have minded his own business.

"Nothing," Esther said. "Peter, please help me to my recliner." Once there, Esther tipped back and slept until everyone was gone. Peter took care of saying goodbye to departing guests.

Chapter 20

Josh came home for the day on Thanksgiving, then was heading back to Kalamazoo after dinner, straight from her mom's home. He didn't even stop by the manse, much to Kathleen's disappointment.

"Couldn't you stay a day or two?" Kathleen asked before he left. "Seems like we never see you."

"Can't Mom. I've got to work the next day."

"Does this have anything to do with the cute blond I hear you've been seeing?" Scott joined the conversation.

"Which one, little bro?" Josh poked Scott on the shoulder. Kathleen frowned.

"Okay, but Christmas, you'll come for Christmas, stay for a few days. You can stay with us."

"What about Stephanie and Michelle?"

"They can share a bedroom. It'll be fun. Please, say you'll stay," Kathleen pleaded.

Josh smiled and gave her a quick hug. "I'll see Mom. I'll let you know later." Kathleen knew what that meant. She wouldn't hear from him for weeks, until she called him.

"What about you, Stephanie? Are you staying a while?" Joe asked his oldest daughter.

"Sorry, Dad. Josh is my ride." Despite the struggles during high school, or perhaps because of them, Stephanie and Josh remained friends. Kathleen knew that if she wanted to know what Stephanie was up to, she need only ask Josh, and vice versa. She was glad her sons and Joe's daughters got along so well. She just wished she saw more of them.

"We'll drive you back, won't we, Kathleen?" Joe suggested.

"Sorry. I've made other plans, Dad. Besides, I have to work tomorrow, too. It's a big day at the mall, black Friday." Stephanie had floundered much like Josh, taking five years to complete her degree.

She was working in a store at the mall and talking about getting a masters in marketing.

"At least we've got Michelle here," Joe put his hand on Michelle's shoulder.

"Sorry, Dad. I'm going back with Josh and Stephanie. I've got too much studying to do and a major paper due next week." Michelle was a junior. At least she was on track to graduate in four years. No sense in doing anything to jeopardize that, Kathleen thought, though she suspected Michelle's desire to go back to the dorm where she was a Resident Assistant had more to do with a male Resident Assistant at the same dorm.

"I guess it's just us," Joe said and put his arm around her side as they watched the kids leave. "It's good we have each other."

"That's the way it is," Peter joined them as they waved their goodbyes. "The young ones move out, leaving us old ones behind."

"Speak for yourself, old man," Joe slapped Peter on the back before saying their goodbyes.

"What happened back there between you and my mom?" Kathleen asked on the ride home. "I never heard her talk like that before."

"I took a shot. I thought I saw an opening and put on my pastor's hat. I guess that's what I get for trying to pastor a family member." Joe had all the pastoral counseling training to explain what had happened. Kathleen was aware of that. He had explained it many times. It didn't make it easier. Kathleen knew that as well. She glanced over at her husband.

"I've never heard my mom speak like that to anyone. It's like she's become a different person. It's not like her. She sounded more like me than her."

"That happens sometimes with strokes. But maybe she's just becoming more honest, more herself," Joe commented.

If that was the case, then Kathleen didn't know her mother after all.

Chapter 21

"You did great yesterday," Peter handed Esther a cup of coffee then sat down next to her in the living room. He had wanted to talk to her last night but she had clearly been too tired. He carefully broached the subject.

"Really? Doesn't seem that way to me."

"Well, there was that incident with Joe."

"What right does he have to preach to me?" Esther stopped, the coffee cup just short of her lips.

"He is a minister."

"Just because he married my daughter doesn't mean he knows anything about me." She set the coffee cup down so she could talk, the cup too heavy for her to hold for long.

"No, of course not. I'm sure Joe would agree with that." Peter took a sip of coffee and tried to come at the topic from a different angle. "You almost seemed your old self at times."

"Really? Because I don't feel like that old self. My old self wouldn't have sat like a helpless lump giving orders while others did the work. My old self wouldn't have slept through half the day." Peter could see this wasn't working.

"But you did okay. Bit by bit, every day you are getting stronger."

"Then you are seeing something I'm not. All I can see is all I can't do. People look at me and they think I'm almost my old self, but I know the difference. I know it's not true. I can hardly remember anything. I have to write notes to myself all the time and then I misplace the notes."

"You remembered what happened between you and Joe."

"Don't try to be funny."

"I'm just saying … Yesterday I thought I saw some of my girl, my Esther, the woman I married."

"Then maybe you're imagining things. You are seeing what you want to see. I don't know who that person was. I don't know who I am. Who am I, Peter?"

"You're the woman I love and will always love. The one I married." How could he make her believe this? Did he believe it himself? Peter searched for the right words. His gut told him the words were true even if Esther didn't believe them, even if his mind questioned.

"Am I? You said yourself, you thought you saw the old me yesterday. What if that old me is gone? What then?"

"I'll still love you. Remember, for better, for worse." Peter set his coffee cup down and reached for her hand.

"And what if the new me doesn't love you anymore?" Esther stared down at the hand on hers but didn't move.

"Is that true?" He didn't believe it. Felt deep inside that it wasn't true. He knew the Esther he had married, the Esther he loved, was still inside this woman. How to get her to realize it?

"I don't know. I don't know anything anymore. I don't know myself, don't recognize myself. How can I love anyone when I don't even know who I am?"

Peter kept hold of her hand.

"Do you love the me I was or the me I am?" Esther asked.

He squeezed her hand, lightly caressing her hand with his thumb as he considered his response. "Both." He paused. "I'm willing to give the new you a chance."

"Peter, what if I never fully recover? What if I'm never myself again?" Esther's shoulders dropped and she shook her head as she spoke.

"Then we'll find a new normal together."

"All I've ever known, all I've ever done was take care of others. Who am I now that I can no longer do that? I can barely take care of myself. Who am I now that others have to take care of me?" She stared at him as if he had the answer. What could he say?

"You are still the woman I love."

84

"Really? I wish I could believe that." She pulled her hand away from his.

"Believe this," Peter took both of her hands in his. "I'm here and I'm here to stay. You can't push me away so easily. I love you and we will get through this together. That's what marriage is about."

Esther tried to wipe away a tear with her right arm. She failed. Peter reached over and wiped it for her with his hand then kissed her gently on her lips.

Esther always had to get home to take care of Bobby. Even after her mother returned to her old self, she helped with Bobby. It was what she did. Bobby was a sweet, sickly boy. Not like other boys she knew. She always knew he was special. When he was diagnosed with leukemia at age five, she had already spent the last five years of her life taking care of him, so this was no difference, only more so. Her life, her family, all revolved around Bobby and his care. She knew not to ask for anything for herself. Knew what the answer would be. While other girls were playing hopscotch and jump rope, she was cleaning up puke after chemo treatments. Her father was her only ally in taking time for herself to be a child. He would send her outside on the weekend when he was home, encourage her to have friends over.

"What's wrong with your brother?" The question always came up.

"Nothing. He's just sick." She couldn't bring herself to mention the big C, cancer, or leukemia. She didn't want to be branded as the girl with the sick brother. When she made a friend, they rarely stuck around. Who wanted to play with a friend who always had excuses for why she couldn't come out or have friends over? No, she was better off in the cocoon of her family.

The exception was playing tennis. Her dad had bought Esther her first tennis racket. He took her to the courts and taught her.

"She has to get out of this house sometimes, Carolyn. You can't keep her trapped in here forever," her dad told her mom.

"But who will help me with Bobby? I can't do it by myself."

"You'll be fine for a few hours." Her dad had acted in an unaccustomed manner in putting his foot down. Esther loved him for it. She loved their Saturday afternoon tennis lessons and soon excelled at the game. She never joined the tennis team in high school, but was able to participate in the summer programs put on by parks and recreation.

Esther didn't mind staying with Bobby. Together they created their own world. While Esther was at school, Bobby read adventure books. He was always ready with new stories to share when she came home. They would be pirates in the South Seas.

"Avast ye hardies," Bobby would say and draw an imaginary sword.

"Aye, aye, captain." Esther was always his first mate, right hand guy, gal Friday.

They explored the darkest jungles of Africa after Bobby read *Jungle Book*, were shipwrecked on a deserted island after he read *Treasure Island*. Esther believed the adventures would never end.

She was actually disappointed when he would go into remission and return to school. She was jealous of anyone who sought to enter their private world. She watched for him at lunch time and during recess to make sure no one picked on his frail body. She needn't worry. Bobby captivated his classmates with his stories as much as he captivated her. While other boys were "wrassling," climbing the monkey bars, and playing tag, Bobby held court, sitting on a picnic table and making up stories for his audience. He made up the stories that others acted out under his direction. He always ended with a cliff-hanger, leaving them begging for more.

"Stay tuned till tomorrow," he would say with a smile as he climbed off the table and carefully made his way back to the classroom. Even when in remission he remained frail and bruised easily. He accepted his lot with a wisdom reserved for those who had confronted death, even though a child. Though he was four years her junior, he was older in maturity and life experience.

Esther liked being his side-kick. On those days he wasn't well enough to attend school, she would bring his backpack home filled with his homework. He worked to keep up with his studies so he didn't fall behind his class. Even when tired, he always had a smile and a story for her.

Their mother wasn't a part of this magical world. She remained on the fringes where she cried and fretted with every relapse, real or imaginary. Esther knew even then, that she was the stronger of the two, that it wasn't just Bobby who needed taking care of, but her mother.

Her dad got glimpses into their world. He would peek into the room, see that they were both awake and ask them what mischief they were up to.

"When you're old enough, son, you and me, we're going to join the French foreign legion," he would tease. "Leave these women to their female ways."

"And what about me?" Esther would stamp her foot and snarl at him.

"I guess you could come along ... as cook," Bobby would say and laugh. Esther didn't mind being side-kick, but cook ... no, that was not for her.

"Don't worry, Esther. You'll be off having adventures of your own, better ones. Ones we mere men wouldn't understand," her dad insisted.

Then her mother would come in and break up the party.

"Are you still up? Erick, what are you doing? You know Bobby needs his sleep. And you, too, Esther. You know better than to keep your brother up."

Esther did know better. Sometimes Bobby struggled to sleep or woke up in pain. She would hear a soft moan escape his lips. Bobby was so brave but he couldn't keep up the front he put on for his mother all the time. He tried not to let his mother know when he was in pain, but Esther could tell. She could tell by the strain in his voice and the tightness in his jaw. She would sneak into his room at night and lay by his side until he fell asleep.

"Don't worry, little brother, I'm here," she would whisper.

"Don't tell Mom."

"No, I won't. It'll be our secret."

"Because you know how Mom is."

They played out this routine for seven years, with Bobby getting sick, going to the hospital, then coming home in remission. Each remission brought renewed hope for a full recovery, until the last time.

Esther had rushed to Bobby's room, eager to tell him about tennis and the blond-haired boy. Her dad was calling an ambulance, her mother was crying and cleaning up blood from the bathroom floor. Bobby smiled wanly at her from his wheel chair. He was still in his pajamas, wrapped in a blanket.

"Sorry, sis. Guess it's time."

"No, it's not." They had talked about this before, talked about when it would be time for him to leave. Or rather Bobby talked, Esther refused to listen. She didn't want to let him speak nonsense.

"Don't say such things. You're better. You're going to continue to get better. And someday we'll both get married and have children and our children will play together."

"Esther, you know that's not true. Even if you can't admit it now, you know in your heart."

"No, I don't know. And if you loved me, you wouldn't talk to me this way." She hated it when he talked like this. Her stomach ached and churned at the same time.

"I have to talk to someone. You know I can't talk to Mom or Dad. If you loved me, you would let me talk." She knew that. She had to ignore her gut and listen.

"Okay, talk, but I don't have to accept what you say."

"When the time comes, when it's time for me to go. I want you to remember how much I love you. I'll always be with you, in your heart, in that beautiful big heart. You will need to be strong for Mom. Tell her I understand."

"What do you understand?"

"I know how hard this has been on her."

"On her. What about me?" Why was it always about her mom? Esther wanted to be angry but she couldn't. Not where Bobby was concerned. How could she be angry at him?

"You'll be fine, sis. Tell her. Promise me. I don't want any sad farewell. Can you do that for me?"

"I'll try. But by then, you'll be an old man, with children and grandchildren. You're going to outlive me, baby brother."

She hadn't been able to accept what he was saying, any more than she had been able to accept the reality of Dale's death. Both were crushing weights on her heart.

"You will come back from this stronger, sis. I know you. I know you will," Bobby had whispered to her before he died.

"How can I? My heart is broken beyond repair," she wanted to say, but there was no one to listen. Bobby, Dale, her mom. All were gone.

"Those broken spots will always be there, but they will heal. They will make you stronger. Hearts are made for love. Your heart was made for love. The heart's capacity for love only grows larger with each loss." Was it Bobby, speaking those words in her dreams, or Dale? The two losses became as one in her post-stroke dreams.

She hadn't believed the words, but they were true. Her dreams of a large family had been broken, just like her mother's dreams, but unlike her mother, she became stronger.

Bobby didn't come back from the hospital this time. He had been right. She hadn't wanted to tell Dale, kept putting him off. He kept reminding her of her promise.

She continued to play tennis. Her father had insisted on it.

"You can't be here all day in this hospital You need to get out, get fresh air."

She and Dale became doubles partners. While on the courts and with Dale, she managed to push away her worries about Bobby.

"Where do you slip away after our games?" Dale asked her. "Why don't you let me drive you?"

"I don't slip away. I have to go home."

"No, you slip away, even before you leave. I see your eyes. They go somewhere in your head, where I can't follow. Somewhere sad. Tell me, my Queen Esther. Where do you go?"

"No place in particular." Esther avoided his gaze.

"Okay, for now, but you will tell me someday, won't you? When you are ready."

Esther didn't respond, choosing to slip away to the hospital.

After every match, Dale asked her out. When she continued to turn him down, he offered to drive her home.

"Hey, you still owe me that ice cream float, remember. I hate to drink alone."

"Now's not a good time." How could she tell him about Bobby now? What would he say? Just the thought brought tears to her eyes. If she let the tears start, would she ever be able to stop them?

"Will there ever be a good time? I'm patient, but I know when I'm not wanted. If you aren't interested just say so." Dale stared at her. When she didn't answer he shook his head. "Okay. I'm out of here," he started to walk away.

"Wait," Esther's voice was barely audible. She didn't know why, but she felt like her world was walking away from her. With him was going a part of her heart, but how could she say that? How could she tell him? When Dale didn't stop, she raised her voice, "Wait. Don't go."

Dale turned around. "And why should I stay? Give me a reason."

"Because my brother is in the hospital and if I lose you too, I couldn't bear it."

Dale hurried back to her. "Your brother, in the hospital?"

"Yes, leukemia. They don't think he's going to make it."

"Why didn't you tell me?"

"Because … because of this, this conversation. I didn't want to have it, talk about it. Everyone at school knows about my brother. It was nice having someone who didn't know, who didn't look at me with sad, pitying expressions. They say they are sorry, then they leave to never talk to me again. It's not like it's contagious, or like I have cancer. But because my brother does, my family has cancer. No one wants to be around someone who is dying. I thought you wouldn't want to be with me if you knew." The tears slid out, just as she had feared. But Dale didn't run away.

"Then you thought wrong. You would have deprived me of meeting your brother, getting to know him while I still can. How selfish of you."

"What do you mean?" Esther sniffled. What was he talking about? Her selfish? The words broke through her wall of tears.

"I want to meet your brother, right now, while I still can."

"Now? Are you sure?" What was he saying? Did he know what he was asking?

"Yes, now. And your dad and mom too. I want your brother's permission to date his sister."

Dale went to the hospital with her that day, and every day until the end. Bobby liked him. He told her so after that first visit.

"Can I have a word with my sister, alone?" he told Dale. "He's a good one, sis. He's right for you," he said after Dale left.

"How do you know? You only just met him."

"Trust me. As your older brother, I know about these things."

"You aren't older than me."

"In years, maybe, but in wisdom, I'm way older than you." Esther shook her head and laughed.

"You keep telling yourself that—"

"— because it's true."

"If you think so, but I'll always be your big sister."

She didn't tell Dale what Bobby had said, at least, not till years later, when they were married, late one night, lying together in bed.

"Can't sleep?" Dale had asked as she tossed and turned.

"Just thinking," she said.

"About what?"

"About Bobby, that first day you met him." She turned toward him and raised her head on her hand in order to see him better in the shadows.

"What about it?"

"What he said. He said you were the right one for me. He was right. You are the right one for me. I wonder how he knew." She continued to seek out the outline of his face.

"What's not to like?" Dale teased and reached for her, pulling her close. "I knew you were the one for me the day we met, when you slammed that tennis ball almost down my throat."

"Really?"

"Yes, really. Every day after that just confirmed it."

Esther fell back to sleep, safe in his arms.

Chapter 22

Much as Kathleen hated to see the kids go, she was also glad for this time with Joe. No church meetings this weekend because of Thanksgiving. They had two whole days to themselves until Sunday and the obligatory service. Kathleen was also excused from the traditional Friday after Thanksgiving putting up storm windows and getting the house ready for winter at her mom's. Peter had finally talked her mom into having new, energy-efficient windows installed. There were no such projects at the manse since the maintenance of the building was taken care of by the church building and grounds crew.

"See, another perk of living for free in the manse," Joe told her. She had to agree on this one. They sat in the kitchen with their coffee the next morning.

"What's on the agenda for today?" Joe asked.

"Nothing. Isn't that wonderful?"

"Then why did we even bother to get out of bed? What are we doing in these clothes?" Joe teased, stood up and got ready to go back upstairs.

"There's something I want to talk to you about," Kathleen said.

"Uh-oh," Joe sat back down. "That doesn't sound good."

"It's nothing. It's just, I haven't had a period for three months."

"Oh," no other word came out of Joe's mouth as he sought the right one. Kathleen could see him picking and choosing his words. "You're not …?"

"I don't know. My periods have never been that regular. But I've never gone this long between periods."

"Don't you think we should check it out?"

"I guess. I wanted to talk to you first."

"What's there to talk about? First, we find out what's going on, then we talk."

"Okay, I guess …" Kathleen stared down at her coffee, unwilling to meet his gaze.

"What's the matter?"

"I'm sorry. I know you didn't want any more kids." She continued to avoid his eyes.

"I never said that." Joe took her hands in his.

"Yes, you did. I'm not sure how this happened."

"Honey, we both know how this happens. Have you been taking your birth control pills?"

"Yes … er, mostly. Sometimes I forget. I'm sorry."

"Nothing to be sorry about. First, we find out if you are pregnant. It could be menopause." How could Joe be so calm about this? What was going on in that head of his?

"No way! I'm too young for that." Kathleen looked up at him at the suggestion.

"You are forty-four. Some women enter menopause that early."

"But not me," though she did wonder about a slow rush of heat that had crept over her body the other day at dinner. Could that have been a hot flash? No, she was sure it would be more dramatic than that. And besides, she was way too young.

"We can get a pregnancy test today, this morning."

"Okay." Kathleen agreed.

"What's wrong?"

"I don't know what's wrong. This is not exactly how I envisioned spending this time together." It wasn't how she envisioned her life, period, but here she was, living in a church manse with a minister and maybe, could it be … pregnant? She wasn't sure what she thought about it.

"I'll get ... no, wait. Maybe we better drive to some place where they don't know us." Joe was right. Kathleen imagined the gossip network being activated the minute either one of them picked up a pregnancy test. "We'll make a day of it. Go out for lunch, maybe see a movie. Don't worry. Everything will be all right."

"Unless it isn't."

"Kathleen, why do you want to borrow trouble?"

Because that's what I do, Kathleen thought to herself. Wherever I go, trouble follows. And now I've brought my trouble to Joe. At least they were in this together.

Kathleen went upstairs to get ready, leaving Joe to clean up from breakfast. She was back downstairs shortly afterwards.

"Why aren't you ready?" Joe asked.

"Because we don't have to go." Kathleen put forth a bravado she didn't feel.

"What are you saying?"

"I'm saying, my period started. I knew I had been feeling off, just didn't know why. No reason to get a pregnancy test now."

"Are you okay?" Why did he have to be so nice? Her façade fell away and she started to cry. Joe pulled her over to him, sat her down at the table next to him and put his arm around her shoulder as she sniffled.

"I don't know. I don't want a baby, but now that I know I'm not having one …" Kathleen's voice cracked.

"You know, we can start trying, to have a baby that is. If that's what you want." Joe continued to hold her.

"No, that's not what I want. I should be relieved. I don't know what's wrong with me. I just, I don't want that door to be closed."

"It's not closed."

"Not yet. But soon it will be, sooner rather than later."

"Then we better talk more about this sooner, not later." He pulled her closer. "Besides, the process of getting pregnant is fun. We can have lots of fun while we sort this out."

Kathleen laughed despite her fears and held Joe close. Too many changes.

This time when her period came, it came with a vengeance. The flow was so heavy she had to change her pants several times. When she talked to her gynecologist about it, she told her she was going through perimenopause.

"That happens. You might go for months with no period, then have a spotty one, or might have excessive flow."

"People talk about menopause all the time, but I haven't heard anything about perimenopause."

"Oh, it's real. Like menopause, it's different for everyone. Some women have no symptoms, others have symptoms like yours. Have you had any hot flashes yet?" Dr. Phelps asked as she listened to Kathleen's chest.

"I think I might have."

"You'll know when it happens. Any questions?" She put her stethoscope down in order to give Kathleen her full attention.

"Can I still get pregnant, that is if I want to get pregnant?"

"Sure. Lots of women have babies in their forties. There's all those 'oops' babies. Just when the kids have left the nest, surprise, along comes another baby."

"I don't know that I want that." Oops. That didn't sound good.

"Then we can talk about it."

"But what if I do?"

"We can talk about that too."

Kathleen sighed. Talk. What good was talk?

Chapter 23

"Can't we just skip Christmas this year?" Esther asked.

"But you love …" Peter started. Esther shot him "that look", shutting him down. He knew better. She just wasn't up for Christmas. "What about a tree? Don't you want a tree? Dale will cut one for us if we ask him." Peter took a different tactic. She recognized the ruse.

"Okay," she would give him this one. A tree might be nice. Especially a live one. "A small one. No need to get the large artificial one out." Esther always had two trees. The artificial one went up after Thanksgiving and sat in her living room where it withstood the onslaught of grandkids. The live tree enjoyed a prominent place in the kitchen where she could enjoy it while sipping coffee in the morning and while cooking. The smell of pine needles mixed in with the smell of cooking. This year she would put the live tree in the living room. "But nothing else. No garlands, no candles or other decorations."

"No wreath?"

"We have to have a wreath."

"No manger? We have to have a manger."

"No manger." She was not on good terms with Jesus right then, not even baby Jesus.

"Okay, just a tree and wreath," Peter agreed.

"And no Christmas service or Christmas dinner." She knew she was pushing it, but too bad. If Peter didn't like it, too bad.

"You know your kids are going to invite you to their homes."

"No, not going. It's just another day. Dad can go. You can take him. But not me." Peter agreed but she knew it wasn't over. She knew there would be pressure from all sides.

"We'll see. You might change your mind," Peter said. Esther decided not to challenge him on this. It took too much energy.

Her first husband, Dale, had loved Christmas. The candle-light Christmas Eve service, the music, giving presents. He had loved everything about it. Holiday music filled the house from Thanksgiving to Christmas whenever he was home. He loved buying gifts for others. He didn't care about gifts for himself. She had always struggled to come up with the right gift, often failing miserably.

He always found the biggest tree that would fit in the living room. Even when they had little furniture, that first year, he spared no expense on the tree. Kathleen remembered that first Christmas in this house. Kathleen had been a baby. What furniture they had was from her parents' home — a beat-up couch and a brown recliner. Their moving out had been just the excuse her mom had been waiting for to get new furniture. They used crates for end tables and a coffee table, long before it had become stylish. Back then it had been about necessity, not style.

But they had the tree Dale had insisted on, filling one quarter of the living room. Dale strung the lights and she had put on the few ornaments they had — wedding gifts, a box from her parents' tree that they had passed on to her and the few she had bought. They had strung popcorn and cranberries to help fill all of the bare spaces, then sat and admired their handiwork and talked about their dreams. Kathleen was turning over but had not yet learned to creep. That was the first and only Christmas they had been able to put her in one place and expect her to still be there. Once Kathleen started creeping, it wasn't long till she pulled herself up to stand. She never stayed still after that, always moving, running away from her as quickly as her little legs would carry her.

Over the years the ornaments and decorations had grown till now they filled several boxes, packed away in the attic. Esther instructed Peter as to which box to get down.

"We don't need a lot of decorations," she reminded him. Peter loved Christmas too. She felt bad about depriving him of Christmas, but not so bad to change her mind. Besides, he wasn't big on the decorations of Christmas. He liked the food and family part of the holiday. Presents didn't matter to him either. They had agreed early on to not worry about buying gifts for each other.

"Instead of gifts, let's gift each other with trips and special experiences," Peter had suggested. Esther had agreed in principle, though had yet to follow through, resisting leaving her home and family. So far, they had travelled to Florida for a month the last few winters but that was it. When was she going to make good on all of those promises now?

Still, handling Peter was nothing in comparison to handling Kathleen. Seemed she had been battling Kathleen since Kathleen was born. Why should now be any different? She knew skipping Christmas would be another battle with Kathleen.

"Of course, you are coming to Dale's for Christmas dinner," Kathleen had insisted. "It won't be Christmas without you."

"It will still be Christmas."

"It won't be the same. You don't want to disappoint your grandchildren."

Esther knew Kathleen would play the grandchild card eventually. Kathleen wasn't going to win this one.

"The grandkids will be fine without me." She was surprised when Kathleen backed down. What was that girl up to now?

Chapter 24

"Have you ever thought about having another baby?" Kathleen asked Julia during their lunch date.

"No, have you? You aren't pregnant, are you? Because that would be amazing!"

Why did she decide to bring this up? She regretted it already. But Julia was her best friend. If she couldn't talk to her best friend about this, who could she talk to? If only Julia didn't gush so.

"No, I'm not. I was just wondering if you had thought about it."

"You're thinking about it, though. I'll be the godmother. I'll make an awesome godmother."

"There's no baby, Julia. Answer the question."

"I guess I haven't thought about it. Too busy. How would I find time for a baby? Besides I'm not married. You and Joe though …"

"Please. Don't go there."

"You must be thinking about it or you wouldn't have asked."

"Okay. We have talked about it. I am thinking about it. I just don't know. This is my last chance to try again and maybe do it right. Not that Josh and Scott didn't turn out right. It's just that says more about my mom than me since she raised them when they were little."

"And you may do everything right and still have a problem child."

"I know. I wasn't exactly exemplar as a child growing up." Kathleen frowned as she remembered some of what she had put her mother through. Did she really want to risk dealing with that?

"But you turned out okay, eventually."

"Eventually. What if I have a daughter and she turns out like me?"

"Would that be so bad?"

"It would be terrible. I couldn't handle another me. The world couldn't handle another me." Of that, Kathleen was sure. She wouldn't entertain the possibility.

"What if you had a daughter and she's everything you could have hoped for and more?"

"Get real. That doesn't happen."

"Well, Alex …"

"Okay. I'll give you that. Alex is great." Kathleen had to agree to that. Alex would be a great daughter-in-law, if … The thought was a pleasant one.

"And look at your nieces, Ashley and Grace."

"Ashley …?"

"Okay, Grace then. Besides, it may be a boy. Don't you think Joe would like a son?"

"Why are we even talking about this?" Kathleen picked at her food. Why had she gotten this salad? What had she been thinking? She should have gotten her usual bacon cheeseburger. She pushed the salad away.

"You brought it up." Julie looked at the salad that remained uneaten on Kathleen's plate. "Not hungry?"

"I just don't know what I want. And if I wait too long, it'll be too late."

"Plenty of women have babies in their forties," Julia assured her.

"Is that what you are waiting for?"

"I thought this was about you."

"I asked you first."

Julia put her fork down and thought. "Okay. Like I told you before. I'm not the marrying type. I'm married to my work. And if I'm not married, why would I consider having a baby? I know what it's like to be a single parent. I don't need to do that again. No, if I have another baby, I want someone else to help me."

"Someone like Henry. He'd be a great father."

"And Joe. He'd be a great father." Julia was not going to let her off the hook.

"So, what are we waiting for?" Kathleen paused for effect. "Let's see. Nine months of pregnancy, not being able to drink, nausea, and then labor, followed by a minimum of eighteen years before they are on their own. Do you realize how old I'll be by then? Why would anyone want to put themselves through that?"

"Right," Julia agreed. "Why should we have babies when we have kids old enough to have babies? It's their turn."

"Yes, they can make us grandmothers so we can have all the fun and none of the responsibilities."

"Right, time for them to get busy," Julia said, then added, "Wait, what am I saying? Do I really want to be a grandmother? Am I really old enough?"

"Yes, you are. We both are."

"Okay. Here's to being a grandmother, but not just yet."

"I'll drink to that!" Kathleen said as they clinked glasses. She was in no hurry to be a grandmother.

Chapter 25

Her first Christmas as a married woman. Why wasn't she excited? She had a husband who was busy with planning Christmas services and a mother who had decided to skip Christmas this year, that's why. This Christmas was not off to a good start. Not what she had imagined her first Christmas as a married woman to be. She had known Christmas without family in the past. She knew what that was like. Those years in Chicago when Christmas had come and gone without her taking notice. Christmases while in jail. No decorations or gifts. All she had gotten was the Christmas cards her mother had sent that she kept in her cell. She attended the service just to get out of her cell block. No, Christmas with family was so much better.

Her brother Dale and his wife Ava were having family over for Christmas dinner. Josh, Stephanie and Michelle were coming home for the day. Stephanie and Michelle were staying in their old rooms, Josh staying at her mom's. Josh, Scott and Alex were coming over for breakfast Christmas morning, then Scott and Alex were going to Alex's mom's while they went to Dale's. Kathleen went through the schedule in her head. Sigh. One day and then they would be gone, going back to their real life. The next day Joe and she were driving to Joe's parents for a few days. It wasn't ideal, but she would take what she could get. Didn't mean she had to like it.

The manse continued to feel like she was an unwelcome intruder. It just wasn't home. The addition of a Christmas tree and decorations did little to help.

The arrival of the Women's Guild with cookies and hot cocoa, followed by the church janitor lugging boxes was not a welcome surprise.

"We're here to decorate the manse," the president of the Women's Guild announced. "Didn't Pastor tell you?" she asked as Kathleen stood in the doorway blocking their entrance.

"No, he didn't say anything about it."

"It's a tradition. We always decorate the manse for Christmas. You don't mind, do you? We brought cookies!"

"No, I don't know. I guess not," Kathleen had stumbled for the right words.

"Good." The women pushed past her.

Kathleen escaped to the kitchen and called Joe. "Joe, the Women's Guild is here. Something about decorating the manse?"

"Oh, didn't I tell you? They do it every year. It's not a problem, is it?"

"Not for them, but for you it is," Kathleen told him in her "wait till you get home" voice. She imagined Joe squirming on the end of the other line. Good, let him worry.

"Sorry, honey. Do you want me to tell them to go away?"

"And make me into the bad guy. No."

"Okay, I guess we'll discuss this when I get home."

"Yes, we will." Kathleen slipped out of the house. She was glad to have Joy's Center for her escape. At least there she had some say in what Christmas decorations were put up.

"Don't you want to help?" The president called after her.

"Sorry. I have to get to work," Kathleen responded.

"We'll save some cookies for you and Pastor."

"Good, you do that," Kathleen said as she climbed into her car.

They were the church's decorations, not hers, not theirs, hers and Joe's. Nothing to uniquely claim the season as their own as a couple. When the members of the Women's Guild were done, there were decorations throughout the first floor of the house, including the bathroom. Artificial trees in the sitting room, living room and rec room in the basement. Each tree had a different theme. Garlands were strung throughout the house and Christmas knick-knacks in every spare space. How many Christmas creches could one house hold? There were large ceramic ones under each tree, miniature Christmas ornaments hanging from tree branches, simple three-piece ones, featuring Mary, Joseph and Jesus on every ledge, and ones with

104

elaborate menageries filling and overflowing the stable on every table. And then wreaths and candles. The women had sprayed artificial pine smell to cover the mustiness from being stored away in a closet somewhere.

Joe was far too busy with church to take time to go tree hunting. She had accepted that. She was busy as well with the Christmas recital at the dance studio. But even with that, she had far too much time alone in the manse — it just wasn't home.

Home was the house she had grown up in. Even during her wayward youth, while in Chicago and then as a resident of the Cook County jail system, that house remained home. Her one true home. The places she had slept had just been somewhere to lay her head, temporary lodging while on her journey to her real home. She had been restless, when she stopped long enough to realize it. She had resisted living in her mother's home when she had first moved back to Cascade Falls, had dreamt of a home of her own, moving out, but now that she had, she missed having coffee with her mom and Peter and her grandfather every morning. She missed the high school years of Josh and Scott and the energy they had brought into the house. At least now she had Joe, but this building was not what she had dreamt about. Maybe having the kids home for Christmas will help. Would this place ever feel like home? What would it take to make it a home?

Chapter 26

Joe brought a potted live fir tree home that night.

"I'm so sorry. I had completely forgotten about the Women's Guild decorating the manse. They do it on the first Monday in December. They've been doing it for years. The girls never minded. I didn't think about it."

"And if you had, would it have made a difference?" Kathleen asked.

"Of course, it would have. I'd have told them we want to decorate our home ourselves."

"You really would have? You're not just saying it?" Kathleen didn't believe him.

"I really would have," Joe hugged her. "You're the most important person in my life now. I know I can get caught up in my work and seem to forget it. Sometimes I need reminding. But you are more important to me than the church, the Women's Guild or the hospital."

"Just so you don't forget it."

"I suspect you won't let me." Joe kissed her then added, "But then, what's not to like about someone else doing all of the work of decorating. I mean, you do like multiple trees, garish lights and enough knick-knacks to overflow onto the floor and cover the coffee table so that there's no room for your coffee cup. I know I do." Joe waved his hand about the room as he spoke, indicating all of the decorations.

"I love you, but this …," Kathleen shook her head and pointed at the display, "No!"

Joe laughed. "We can remove a few items, enough to have a space for our tree."

"And risk offending someone?"

106

"They won't be offended if they don't know." All of the meetings that had been scheduled for the manse had been moved to the church hall except for the youth group. "We can't move the pool table and ping pong tables to the church," Joe had explained.

Kathleen had agreed to the youth group. She liked the young energy they brought to the house.

"All it takes is for one of them to show up with a casserole or cinnamon rolls, looking for an opportunity to snoop."

"Okay. So, what are we going to do with our tree?"

"We'll put it upstairs, away from prying eyes, and decorate it with the ornaments we received as wedding gifts. After Christmas we can move it downstairs."

"And when we get a home of our own, we can plant it in our yard." Joe hugged her again and whispered in her, "I promise, next year will be different. I'll tell them we want to decorate ourselves."

"Yes, you will, because if you don't, I will, and I won't be as tactful as you." She laughed and added, "What did I do to deserve someone like you? Or maybe, what did you do to deserve someone like me? God must be punishing you for something."

"No, we're meant for each other. You're an eight to my five."

"What are you talking about?"

"The Enneagram. Don't you remember? We did the questionnaire before we got married." Oh, those. She didn't really remember. Joe loved doing personality profiles. Her, not so much. She only filled them out because it was important to Joe.

"Was that the one with all the letters? GBTE or whatever?"

"No, that was Meyers-Briggs. And your letters are ESTJ."

"You remember that?"

"You don't?"

"Guess it wasn't that important to me." Kathleen shrugged her shoulders.

"The Enneagram is numbers, numbers associated with personality traits. I've been reading about Harmony Triads."

"You've lost me."

"They are the three numbers associated with harmony and wholeness."

"I still don't get it."

"Here," Joe pulled out a book with a picture of the nine points of the Enneagram on it. "See how these numbers form a triangle."

"Yeah." Where was he going with this?

"You're an eight and I'm a five, the thinker, analyzer."

"You're right about that." Joe took time to think about everything, down to the last little detail. It took him forever to "reflect" on every decision before making a choice, if he made a choice. It was annoying. Why couldn't he just go with his gut, like she did. She did what seemed right and worried about the consequences later. Kathleen paused. And how was that working for her, she asked herself?

"Our triangle is two, five, eight. For harmony, I need to embrace my eight more."

"Sounds like a good idea to me." Kathleen playfully hugged him. Wouldn't it be great if Joe wouldn't agonize so about decisions, be more like her? "And maybe I need to think more before just doing what I want, embrace my 'inner five'," Kathleen teased.

"That's not a bad idea, but for harmony, you need to move towards the two."

"What does that mean?" Now what? Where is this going?

"Two is the caretaker. Your mom is a two."

"Oh no. I'm not like my mom, never will be."

"I'm not saying that. You need to embrace your nurturing, caring side more. Put others first sometimes." Where did Joe get this stuff? She knew where. He was always reading, as if he didn't know enough already.

"That's fine for you to say. I already told you, I'm not any good at taking care of others. You knew that about me before we married."

"And I love you. I'm just saying, you are good for me."

"Then why didn't you just say that? Why do you have to add all this other stuff?"

"You bring out the eight in me," Joe said with a smile.

Kathleen put her head in her hand and shook it. What was she going to do about this man?

Chapter 27

Christmas came and went. Esther had remained firm about no Christmas. She had refused to go to Dale's for Christmas dinner, so they had brought Christmas to her.

Esther winced when she opened the gift from Grace. Apparently, she had been planning this gift for a while. She had been worried when she saw the shape, long and narrow with a wide bottom. A cane, like one she had seen at rehab. Grace must have seen it there as well. Hollow, clear plastic, ending with four "feet" for stability. There were pictures up and down the inside of the cane, pictures of her kids and grandkids. Grace must have gone to a lot of work to fix it. Kathleen must have had a hand in it as well.

"Don't you like it, Grandma?" Grace had asked when she hadn't smiled.

"I told you it was a dumb idea," Ashley said.

"Better than your idea … nothing."

"That's what Grandma said she wanted," Ashley defended herself.

Esther hadn't known what to say. The last thing she wanted was a cane, even one with pictures of her kids and grandchildren. Another reminder of all she had lost.

Or maybe a reminder of what she still had. The voice of her mother sounded in her head. "You don't know," Esther told her mother. "You don't know what it's like to be helpless, to not be able to care for your family. To be dependent on others." Esther knew the lie in her words, but held onto them anyway.

She looked at her granddaughters, unsure how to respond. "Grace, it's beautiful," she finally said. "You must have put a lot of thought into this." She couldn't bring herself to lie to her granddaughter, but she also couldn't hurt her with the truth.

Grace came over and hugged her, "I'm sorry if my gift made you sad."

"Oh, no, Gracie. I love it because it came from you."

Now the cane stood next to her chair, unused and unwanted. Was this the new normal? Would she have to accept a life of limited mobility?

Christmas had been better than Kathleen had expected.

"Now it's time for presents," Joe had announced as their kids drove off on Christmas Day.

"I thought I already had my present."

Joe had given her a warm, cushy bathrobe that morning. "To keep you warm in this drafty house," he had said. "What I've bought for under the bathrobe, is just for me to see," he had added.

"Daddy," Stephanie had groaned and rolled her eyes.

"Yeah, really Pastor Joe," Josh had added.

"With that image, I think it's time to go," Scott had excused himself and Alex. Kathleen had laughed as she opened a box with lingerie, closing the box back up before her kids could see.

"That was just the decoy present. Here's the real one." Joe handed her a small rectangular box, just the right size for a tennis bracelet.

"Jewelry?" Kathleen said as she shook the box.

"Open it and see."

Kathleen was surprised by an envelope. Inside the envelope was a gift certificate for a night in Detroit. "A night away?" she asked.

"Not just any night. Look at the date."

"December 31st," Kathleen read. "You mean?"

"Yes, you don't have to go to the hospital New Year's Eve gala this year. We'll spend the night in Detroit, go to one of those clubs you like, maybe go to two or three. Whatever you want to do."

"Joe, this is wonderful," Kathleen said. "But are you sure it's okay to miss the fundraiser? We can always go on another night." They had attended the fundraiser the last few years. The first time, they both had been dating other people. Their dates were now dating each other, Julia and Henry. Since then they still attended because of Joe's involvement with the hospital. They double dated. It wasn't Kathleen's favorite event, but one of those obligatory ones that came with dating a pastor and chaplain. Going with Julia and Henry had made it more palatable.

"No, the reservations are made. Do you have any idea how far in advance you have to reserve rooms for New Year's Eve?"

"But I don't want to cause any trouble."

"Kathleen," Joe took her hands into his and gazed intently into her eyes. "I know you didn't get the wedding you deserve, and then, on our honeymoon you were worried about your mom. And this house … This is one small way for me to make it up to you. I wanted to take you to Chicago but couldn't quite manage two nights. I know how hard it is for you, living here. So, I plan to schedule nights away as often as possible to make our living situations more bearable."

"It's okay, Joe."

"No, it's not. I know this is far from the ideal living situation. And I promise. I'm putting money away every month so we can afford our own home someday. Maybe not this year or the next, but in five years. I have a five-year plan." He squeezed her hands and continued. "I wasn't the best husband in my first marriage. I let my ministry take precedence over my family. I'm not going to let that happen this time."

"It's okay, Joe. I'm not in my twenties with two babies to take care of like Janice was. I'm in my forties and have a life of my own."

"I know, but …," Joe stopped as Kathleen started to cry, tears rolling down her cheeks that she wiped away. "What's wrong? Did I say something wrong?" Joe asked.

"No, what you said, it was perfect. And our wedding, it was perfect too, because it was you and me. That's all that matters."

"Then why are you crying?"

"Because …" Kathleen turned away from him. "I can't believe that I'm saying this, but, I want it all."

"What are you talking about?"

"I want everything. Everything I had rebelled against in my youth. Everything I had insisted I didn't want, would never want. A house, a home, and family, kids. I want a second chance. Maybe I do need to embrace my two."

"What are you saying?"

"Joe, I want to have a baby. I want to have a baby with you. I didn't think I wanted this, but now, I do. Maybe this time I will get it right. I want my kids to know who their father is. I want them to have a mom and dad, not be raised by my mom. Is that too much to ask for?"

"No, not if that's what you want. Then I want it too. I want it for you."

"But it may be too late. My doctor says I'm in perimenopause."

"Then we better get started." Joe picked her up. Kathleen heard his back crack. He set her back down. "Sorry, I guess it is too late for some things." He leaned over, wiped away the remnant of tears on her cheeks and gently kissed her lips, then led her upstairs.

Even the time at Joe's parents had not been too bad. Joe's mother had only cornered her once about having more grandchildren.

"So, have you and Joe talked about kids? You aren't getting any younger," she had said.

"We know, Mom. You don't have to tell us." Joe had intervened.

"I'm just saying. You can father kids at any age, but Kathleen here …," she patted Kathleen's stomach, "Those eggs have a limited shelf life, if you know what I mean."

"She knows what you mean, Mom. Everybody knows what you mean."

"You're so skinny. You need a little fat if you're going to have a baby. Let's see what I can do to put some meat on those bones," Joe's mom added.

Joe shook his head, put his arm around Kathleen and escorted her out of the kitchen into the living room where his father was watching football.

"Looking to escape?" his dad asked.

"You know it," Joe said.

"There's no escaping her. I ought to know. I've tried for fifty years."

"How do you manage?" Kathleen asked.

"A cold brew and a warm TV. Besides, she's a good cook. A man can overlook a lot when his belly's full."

"Then I guess we're in for trouble," Kathleen said with a wry smile. "If good cooking keeps a marriage strong …"

"We'll be just fine," Joe told her and sat down next to her on the couch to watch the game.

"Oh, there's other things, but I don't have to tell you that," Joe's dad winked. Kathleen didn't know which was worse. Both were looking for grandkids. What if she disappointed them?

Chapter 28

Esther gazed around the group of stroke survivors. "I am not here of my own free will," she stated. Her family had run an intervention on her to get her to attend. It was all that minister son-in-law's fault. She was sure he was behind this. He hadn't spoken much, let her family do his dirty work, but she knew he had orchestrated the whole thing.

Esther examined the room. She recognized the young mother, Sally Humphreys, from her stay there, but she was so much improved, Esther didn't want to believe it was her. Why was Sally doing so much better, while she was still struggling? She saw Mr. Potter, the man who couldn't see anything on the left side of his body. Was he still here? Or was he coming on an out-patient basis? He didn't appear to have improved at all. The rest were new to her. Some had been in recovery for months, even years, others were newly admitted to rehab. She determined she would put in her time and go home.

She had known something was up when she saw her family gathered in the living room. Peter, her dad, Kathleen and Joe, Dale and Ava. They even had her grandkids there: Ashley, Jacob and Grace. How dare Joe do this to her!

"We have something to say to you and we need you to listen until we are done," Peter had told her.

"Do I have any choice?"

"Yes, but we'd prefer if you listened." She had nodded her agreement.

"Mom," Kathleen had started. "We are here because we love you and are worried about you."

"You just aren't the same, Mom, and I don't mean the changes because of the stroke. You aren't yourself," Dale added. Esther wanted to interrupt, give him a piece of her mind, but she had been instructed to just sit and listen, so she sat and listened.

One by one they went around the room and told her how much they loved her and how they wanted her to get better.

"We think you are depressed and need help breaking out of that depression. That's why we want you to start attending the stroke support group at the rehab facility," Kathleen said after everyone had their chance to speak.

Was that all they wanted? She thought it was going to be more. She could easily agree to this, if that was all it took to get them off her back.

"We've got it worked out. Peter will take you to the meetings three times a week. If he can't do it, I'll take care of it, or one of us," Kathleen added.

"What do you think, Grace?" Esther asked. Grace had yet to speak up.

"I like the rehab place. I'll go with you, Grandma."

"At least you aren't shipping me off to some hospital or nursing home."

"Why would we do that?" Peter asked.

"I'm not saying you would, but I wouldn't blame you if you did."

"So, you're willing to go to the support group?" Kathleen asked.

"Sure. What do I have to lose?"

Everything. She had already lost so much. What was one more indignity, being dragged to a support group? She would go. Didn't mean she had to participate.

"That went surprisingly well," Kathleen commented on the ride home. Joe had been silent as he thought over the intervention.

"Don't count on it. The real test will be whether she actually goes to the meetings." Joe had plenty of experience with interventions that appeared to go well, the person giving the appearance of agreeing just to get it over with, then not following through, signing themselves out of rehab or refusing to participate once there. But then, that had been interventions with addicts. It had been Kathleen's idea to try an intervention on her mom. "She may have just been going along with what we asked with no intention of actually doing it."

Joe had questioned running an intervention on Kathleen's mom. "As long as it's done right, I guess it won't hurt."

"And if not done right?"

"The person can feel betrayed by family, be angry, get worse."

"All we'll be doing is telling her how much we love her, all of us. How can that hurt? How could that go wrong?"

"You'd be surprised what can happen, but I guess it's worth a try." Joe wasn't confident of his pastoral intuition any more when it came to Esther.

"At least she agreed to go to the meetings."

"Easy to sit in meetings and not participate."

"Now who's inviting trouble? If she keeps going, something good will come of it."

"I hope so," Joe stated. "I hope so," he added under his breath.

Chapter 29

Kathleen and Joe shifted uncomfortably in their chairs. Pictures of babies populated the bulletin board on the wall to their left, overflowing onto the wall. Pictures of family sat on the doctor's desk. Kathleen figured they were his kids. Proof of his fertility. The baby pictures were proof of his ability to do what he claimed he could do — help couples get pregnant. Why didn't she believe them?

Their first visit with the fertility specialist. When Kathleen had talked with her gynecologist about wanting to become pregnant, she had referred her to this man. Perhaps he thought having them meet in his office was better than a cold examination room. He wasn't fooling her.

Kathleen hadn't wanted to go to a specialist. She wanted to stay with her own doctor, a woman doctor with whom she was comfortable.

"Usually I would wait six months to a year before referring a couple, but, because of your age, I recommend you set up the appointment right away," Dr. Phelps had said. "Once you hit forty-five your chance of getting pregnant each month is only three percent. With your irregular periods, it's probably less. You could try charting your cycle, learning how to recognize when you are ovulating and most fertile. That's something you can do right away, but I still recommend a specialist."

"Can't you just give me some drugs to make me fertile?"

"I could, but I really think the best course is to see someone who specializes in fertility. He can check both you and your husband, determine the best course of treatment."

And so, here they were. They had opted to see a specialist out of town in order to avoid any curious eyes.

"If church members see us going to a fertility specialist, it will be all over the church by Sunday," Kathleen said.

"They'll have to know sometime."

"When I'm five months along and no longer able to hide it will be soon enough," Kathleen told him on the drive over.

"What's the process?" Kathleen asked the doctor. "Where do we start?" She had gone on-line and searched as much information as she could, but she wanted, needed to hear it from this doctor.

"The first step is to check both of you. Since you both had children before, that is in your favor. Still, with age, there are complications. If there are no problems that need to be addressed, we may need to juice you with some good drugs to enhance your chance of becoming pregnant." Kathleen had been juiced by drugs before, but nothing like the doctor was proposing. "And if that doesn't work, there's IVF – invitro fertilization, as well as other options."

"And how much will all of this cost?" Joe asked.

"It depends on your insurance and the treatment. Expenses go up with each advance in treatment. We can discuss that once we have a treatment plan in place." The doctor paused to give Joe and Kathleen time to take in the information. Joe squeezed Kathleen's hand.

"Do you need more time?" the doctor asked.

"No, I don't think so," Joe said. "Do we need more time?" he asked Kathleen.

"No, let's get started," Kathleen said, but her voice wavered. She cringed at all those pictures of babies standing in judgment over her.

"Okay then," the doctor stood up. "We'll start by running tests on both of you. See what might be preventing you from getting pregnant."

"Right now?" Joe questioned.

"Right now," he said. "Unless you want more time."

"No, no. That's okay." Joe stood up.

"No, Joe, wait," Kathleen stopped him, grabbing his hand. "Maybe we should think about this."

"If that's what you want."

"Yes, that's what I want." She stood up to leave, still holding Joe's hand. She had to get away from all of those babies.

"Very well then," the doctor said.

Joe pulled loose from Kathleen, shook the doctor's hand and thanked him for his time. "We'll get back to you."

"You do that, but don't take too long."

"I know, I know," Joe told him. He escorted Kathleen out of the office. Kathleen breathed a sigh of relief.

They remained silent for the first part of the drive home.

"What are you thinking?" Joe broke the silence.

"I'm thinking. I'm wondering, how far do we go with this?" Kathleen glanced over at Joe who kept his eyes on the road.

"You heard the doctor. I guess we go as far as we want. As far as you want."

"And how much will it cost?"

"I guess we'll find that out as we go too."

"No. I don't want that. We need to talk about this ahead of time." Kathleen continued to stare at Joe who continued to focus on the road ahead.

"Okay. Talk."

"I thought it was just going to be a matter of me taking some drugs. But now there's tests." She turned her head away from him and gazed ahead at the lines of the highway.

"To see if it's possible for us to get pregnant."

"And then what do we do?" The lines continued to slide by, hypnotizing her as they whirred into the distance.

"If it's not possible?"

"Yes, what do we do?" Is it possible that the highway was dissolving before her as snow began to fall and hinder her sight?

"I guess we look at the options. In vitro?"

"I don't want to do that." She closed her eyes to break the spell of the snow and highway.

"We could adopt."

120

"I don't know that I want to do that either." Her eyes remained closed as she contemplated the options.

"Then, are you sure you want a baby?"

"It was so easy with Josh and Scott. I wasn't looking to get pregnant, wasn't thinking about it at all, and it happened. I thought it would be like that this time. Once we decided we wanted a baby and stopped taking precautions, I thought it would just happen." She spoke as if in a trance, as if speaking only to herself not to a living, breathing entity.

"It could still happen." Joe took his eyes off the road long enough to glance at her. He reached over and squeezed her hand, then quickly put it back on the steering wheel as visibility lessened. Kathleen felt his grasp as if in a dream. She continued to keep her eyes closed as her brain churned out thoughts.

"You heard the doctor. I'm not getting any younger. My doctor told me the chance of someone forty-five getting pregnant is only three percent. I'll be forty-five this summer. I don't like those odds. It may already be too late."

"Or not. All he's talking about are ways to enhance the probability of getting pregnant. Though time is not on our side."

"I know. I just …"

"What?" Joe squeezed her hand again in encouragement.

"I wish I knew what to do, what God would want us to do."

"We can pray about it."

"I have prayed about it. I'm praying now." Kathleen squeezed her eyes tighter.

"And?"

"No answer." Kathleen's voice cracked at the effort to speak. So much easier to remain silent.

"Maybe because we need to be praying together about this." Tears began to slide down Kathleen's check.

"Maybe." They rode in silence for a while. "You know, Joe. This God stuff. This prayer stuff. It's not that easy. It was easier when I just did what I wanted to do." Kathleen opened her eyes and fumbled for a tissue from her purse.

"But was it better?"

"No, I guess not. Still I wonder. Am I still just doing what I want and not what God wants? I want to have a baby, so I go to a fertility specialist."

"We, honey — we went to see the specialist. You keep forgetting that. We are in this together."

"We." Kathleen wiped her eyes. "I guess it's hard for me to accept that. I've been on my own for so long. We. But is this just another way for me to get what I want? I prayed about it, yes, but did I really listen, or am I just trying to use God and prayer to get what I want?"

"Won't be the first-time people have tried to manipulate God. I can assure you, God does not allow himself to be manipulated."

"Maybe God wants me, us, to just trust him. Trust that if it is meant to be, it will be."

"It's okay to help things along. We could do the tests, try the fertility drugs, and then if that doesn't work, accept that it is not God's plan for us."

"We could. Or we could accept whatever God is doing without any intervention."

"Is that what you want?" Joe asked.

Kathleen gazed out at the falling snow, trying to see ahead.

"I don't know. Maybe we can pray about it. Maybe … maybe I'm okay with the way things are. I don't want to close the door to having children. I want to keep it open until God and time close the door. Is that okay?" Kathleen turned towards him as she asked.

"Yes, that's okay."

"Okay, then it's settled." Kathleen turned back away. She was surprised when more tears filled her eyes. "Then why do I feel so lousy?" she asked as she blew her nose.

"Because," Joe reached over and clasped her hand, "maybe it isn't settled. Maybe we do the tests and try the drugs. Is that better?"

122

"Yes, it is." The tears continued but Kathleen did feel better. Joe squeezed her hand again before returning his to the steering wheel.

"I'll call the doctor for an appointment as soon as we get home," he said.

"Okay." Kathleen continued to stare out into the lightly falling snow, unsure of where she was heading.

Chapter 30

Her heart was beating, beating, thump ka thump, ka thump. She was in her heart. She could see it pumping. Then she saw a clump of something break free, traveling through her blood stream, ka thump, ka thump, being pumped into her brain, becoming lodged in her brain, pain. Her heart beat faster, her head ached. She woke up.

"What's wrong?" Peter reached out his arm to where she was sitting straight up in bed.

"I think I'm having another stroke."

Peter sat up beside her, "Are you sure?"

"No, I'm not sure about anything. My heart is beating so hard."

"Slow down, breathe deep. It may be a panic attack brought on by worry over having another stroke." Peter rubbed her back as she tried to catch her breathe.

"My chest feels funny."

"Do you want to go to the hospital?"

"No, I don't. I don't want to. Do you think I should?" A pain erupted across her chest and released in a large burp.

"Wow, what did you eat last night?" Peter continued to rub her back.

"The same as you. Pepperoni pizza."

"I think that's called indigestion. Here, take a Tums." Peter gave her a tablet from the bottle sitting on his night stand. Peter was no stranger to indigestion. He routinely took Tums, almost on a daily basis. She had yet to experience the full range of discomfort associated with indigestion. She had an iron gut, she always said.

Esther took the tablet, chewed it and waited for relief. "I dreamt I saw my heart, saw a clot break loose and head for my brain."

"No more pepperoni pizza for you," Peter said as he lay back down. "Not if it gives you nightmares."

"I don't want to ever go through that again. Not another stroke." Some of the members of the stroke support group told of having second, even third strokes. She continued to sit up, afraid to lie back down. "Peter, promise me, you won't make me go through this again. Just let me go, let me die."

"I don't think that's my call, dear," Peter pulled her down into bed, wrapping his arms around her. "It was just a nightmare. Go back to sleep. Things will look better in the morning."

Esther laid in his arms, listening to him snore. No, it wouldn't be better in the morning. Esther was sure of that. She appreciated the support group, was maybe even getting something out of it despite herself. It was nice to talk to people who understood what she was going through, but their stories … Some had experiences far worse than she. Others less. Some you couldn't even tell had a stroke until they explained how they had changed. And some had repeat strokes. She was afraid of that happening to her as well, being left permanently disabled, in a wheel chair or worse. She didn't want to live if that happened. She had to make Peter understand. He had to pull the plug when the time came.

Peter refused to talk about it that morning. "First, it's not going to happen. Second, if it does, it wouldn't be a matter of pulling a plug but actively ending your life. That I won't, can't do. We'll get through it like we have this." Esther had been afraid of that.

"But if I were on life support, you would pull the plug, wouldn't you?"

"That would be a different story. Most stroke survivors are that — survivors, able to breathe on their own."

"But if I couldn't?"

"I don't want to discuss it any more. Maybe the support group isn't being helpful." Peter reached for the morning paper and hid behind it.

He couldn't be counted on. She would have to make plans herself. But how? How to do it? Should she stockpile pills? Get a gun? But she would have to be able to pull the trigger or put the pills in her mouth and swallow. That might not be an option after a stroke. What was she to do?

"No, I want to keep attending," she told him. Maybe someone there would help her.

Chapter 31

Grace sat down next to Joe in the living room after dinner. Since Esther's stroke, they took turns hosting Sunday dinner for the family. This week it was Dale and Ava's turn. Joe enjoyed this family time, especially now that his daughters were gone.

"Pastor Joe?" Grace asked.

"You can call me Uncle Joe."

"That's okay. I want to talk to Pastor Joe now."

"Oh, okay." Joe turned to face her. What was this about?

"If someone prayed really hard for someone for healing, would God heal that person?"

"That depends," Joe started. "It depends whether it's God's will that the person be healed."

"I don't understand."

"Sometimes there's reasons why God doesn't heal someone. Reasons we don't know or understand. Paul, the apostle, prayed to have an affliction removed, but God didn't remove it. He realized that it wasn't God's will for his life. That sometimes when you are weak, you are strong." Joe saw her eyes glaze over. He recognized this all too well. He was losing her. "Is this about your grandma?"

"No. It's about Josie. Ava says she has Charcout-Marie … something disorder."

"Charcout-Marie-Tooth."

"Yes. It makes me sad. She can't run like the other kids and someday she may have to have braces like her grandmother. If I pray really hard, will God heal her?"

"It's not as simple as that."

"But God can heal her."

"Well, yes."

"Then if he doesn't, he's mean."

"No. That's not quite how it works. You'll understand more when you are older."

"I understand that God can heal Josie, but he doesn't. That's mean."

Joe stared at her intense face. How to respond? How to explain the complexity of suffering in a way a ten-year-old can understand? How to explain something he didn't understand himself?

"But there's so much we don't know or understand. We don't know God's plan for us, or for Josie. There once was a woman named Fannie Crosby."

"Is this a made-up story? Cause I don't believe in fairy tales anymore."

"No, it's real. You can look her up on the internet. She wrote beautiful songs, hymns praising God. Some we sing in our church. 'Blessed Assurance' — you know that song."

"Yes."

"Well she lost her sight when she was just a baby. One preacher remarked on how sad it was that God didn't restore her sight. You know what she said to that?" Grace shook her head no, so Joe continued. "She said that if she had been given one request to make at birth, it would be to be born blind."

"Why would she ask for that?"

"Because she said when she got to heaven, God's face would be the first face she'd see." Joe paused. "And there's another woman, Joni Tada Erickson. She's an artist but she was crippled in a diving accident when she was a teenager, not much older than Ashley. She spent the rest of her life in a wheelchair. She said she'd rather be in a wheelchair with Jesus than walking without Jesus."

"What does that mean? Be thankful for your suffering?" Ashley interrupted. Joe hadn't noticed her sitting in a chair reading.

"It just means, we don't know what God intends for us or for our loved ones. Whatever it is, it's for our own good. What God wants for us is so much better than our own plans. We don't know what God's plans are for Josie. She's lucky she has a friend like you," Joe told

Grace. "She's going to need friends as the disorder progresses. She's lucky to have you."

Ashley rolled her eyes, shook her head and walked out of the room. Clearly, he had not won any points with Ashley over this. He hoped he had helped Grace.

"You keep praying for your friend, Grace," he told her. "And I will too," he added.

Chapter 32

Chloe had to push Ashley to take the lyrical dance class. She didn't understand why Ashley was so resistant. Chloe thought she would jump at the class and had put her name on the list before anyone else.

"What's up, Ashley? Dancing with the Stars? So You Think You Can Dance? They all do lyrical dance. I thought you would love it. And, it's with Letty." Chloe knew Ashely loved Letty. Why the resistance?

"It's just that, I'm into my music. I don't want to take time away from my band."

"It's just three weekends." Chloe put her hands on either side of Ashley's cheeks and stared her in the face. If only she knew what was going on in that head. "Look, Ashley, you are the most talented dancer in the studio. You are the most talented dancer I've come across and that includes Letty. Letty would agree with me. Why are you throwing it away? It's a gift, a gift from God. A gift passed through your mother. Don't throw it away. I understood when you didn't want to continue with step dancing, but this, this, you could make it as a dancer, maybe attend Juilliard. Don't you think you owe it to yourself to give it a try?"

Ashley's blue-grey eyes were clouded, hiding something. Was it thunder clouds, anger? Chloe didn't know what Ashley was hiding behind that stern resolve.

"Now you sound like Aunt Kathleen. I wish everyone would leave me alone, let me be. If I don't want to dance, that's my choice. And if I'm throwing away my God-given talent, that's between me and God." Ashley pulled away from her. "I'm tired of people telling me how gifted I am, how I owe this to my mom."

"You don't owe it to your mom, but maybe you owe it to yourself."

"And maybe I don't want any of it." Ashley started to leave.

"Wait, Ashley. I'm sorry. If you don't want to try it, that's fine. Just think about it first."

"I already have and I'm done thinking about it." Ashley stormed off.

"I'll hold your place open for you," Chloe yelled after her.

Much to her surprise, Ashley showed up at the first class.

"Don't say anything," Ashley told Chloe before she opened her mouth.

"Ashley, I'm so glad you came," Letty hugged her. "Maybe after class we can talk dance, go out for pizza. I'll tell you all about New York."

Ashley didn't respond but Chloe saw a small shift in her shoulders. Maybe she was coming around?

Grace and Josie also showed up.

"I told you, Grace. I'm sorry but you aren't old enough," Chloe told her.

"We just want to watch. I told Josie all about Letty. She wants to meet her. We won't be in the way."

"All right. Stay out of the way." Chloe had wondered what was up with Grace's friend, Josie, when she started attending with Grace. Was it just that she was awkward or was it something more? She sat along the wall and watched while Grace was in class. She watched the dancers' every movement, shifting her shoulders at times as if imitating the movements. When Chloe invited her to give it a try, join the dancers, she hung back and clung to the wall. She knew it wasn't that her parents couldn't afford the lessons. It was something else.

"Do you know Grace's new friend?" Chloe had asked Kathleen after the first week.

"Josie? Sure, sweet kid. Why?"

"She looks like she would like to dance, but when I asked her to join us, she refused. She seems clumsy. Maybe some dance lessons would help."

"I'll see what I can find out," Kathleen told her.

She had been surprised when Kathleen told her she might have a neurological disorder. She wondered, wasn't there something she could do for her? Some way to include her?

Ashley didn't know what the big deal was. Why was Chloe so surprised when she showed up to the dance class? She had said she would think about it, and she did. She wanted to see Letty. This was a good way to do it. She didn't know why it was such a big deal to Chloe and Aunt Kathleen. She didn't care what they said, her focus was her music, the band, not dancing. She didn't care how "gifted" they said she was. She knew about dancing, remembered her mom's sore, bleeding feet. Why would anyone in their right mind want to do that to their body? If she continued with ballet, it was just because … just because. She didn't know why. It somehow seemed wrong to not dance at all. It was her connection to her mom. Nothing more.

She loved playing guitar, pouring out her feelings in her music. She would start with a sad song and after a while her spirits would lift and she'd sing a happy tune. Music never let her down. It was worth the callouses on her fingertips. Better than calloused, bleeding toes. She liked playing in the band, though Caleb was a pain. She put up with him because, technically, it was his band. He had started the group. He just didn't want to admit that she was a better guitar player than him. And sing. She was definitely the better singer, though he was better now that his voice didn't crack. No, music was her avocation, her life. But what did it hurt to try something else? If, when, she made it big, she could use her dance moves to wow the audience. She could go on "The Voice" or "American Idol" and surprise them with her dance moves. That's what she would do.

"Ashley, I'm so glad you came," Letty said as she hugged her. She had almost worried Letty would have forgotten her by now, but then, how could anyone forget her? "You are getting so old? How old are you? Seems like you were nine or ten when I left."

"Eleven. I was eleven when you left. I'm fifteen now. I'm a musician, in a band."

132

"So your aunt told me. I'm glad you decided to take this class."

Ashley shrugged her shoulder to indicate it was no big deal. Her Aunt Kathleen came over, put her arms around Ashley's shoulders.

"Maybe we can get together after class. Catch up, talk dance," Aunt Kathleen said to Letty. Was she including her in this, Ashley wondered? What was Aunt Kathleen up to?

"I'd love too," Letty said.

"Me too," Ashley said, "But won't it be too late?"

"I'll take care of that," Aunt Kathleen said. "Now get out there and dance."

Aunt Kathleen was up to something. She didn't care as long as she got to talk with Letty after class.

Chapter 33

Esther slipped over to get a cup of coffee while waiting for Peter to pick her up after the support group meeting. The coffee was meant to encourage socializing among members. Esther usually tried to slip away without talking to anyone. Too late. She was cornered by Phyllis, the support group leader.

"You don't seem to be getting a lot out of our meetings," she stated as she poured herself a cup of coffee from the large metal urn.

"Why do you say that?" Esther asked.

"You don't participate. You show up, put in your time, then leave."

Esther looked down at her coffee. She wasn't fooling anyone. "My kids think I should attend your meetings."

"What about you?"

"I guess there are worse ways to spend my time."

"Are there?"

Esther squirmed under the woman's firm yet kind gaze. She didn't answer.

"How are you getting on?" Phyllis continued her questioning.

"How am I supposed to be getting on? You tell me, then I'll fake it so everyone will feel better and leave me alone."

"But what about you? What will it take for you to feel better?"

"Hah," Esther turned away from the woman. "The impossible. To be fully functional and get back all that I lost. I guess that's not in the stars."

"No, you won't regain full mobility. Your life has changed, but you can find a new normal."

Esther turned back to face her. "New normal, new normal. People keep saying that. You have to find a new normal. What is that? What if I don't want a new normal? The old normal was just fine."

"But it's gone."

"What's normal anyway?" Esther shrugged her shoulders.

"You tell me. What's normal to you?"

"To me? To get up, make coffee for myself and my family, fix breakfast, do the laundry. I just want to be able to take care of the people I love. Is that too much to ask?"

"You can't do that now? You seem to be getting around pretty well."

"Not that way I want to. The way I used to." Esther sighed. "I can do it some, I guess, but I get tired so quickly, and I still mess up recipes. I can't remember. I turn on the stove then walk away and forget about it until the fire alarm goes off. Peter doesn't want me to cook anymore because of it. If I can't feed my family, what good am I?"

"That's something we can work on. We can work on your memory, your cooking skills. That's something you can relearn, if you want to."

"Why wouldn't I want to?" Esther looked at the woman. What was she talking about?

"Oh, I don't know. I'd kind of like the break from cooking myself. Might be nice to let someone else do that now and then."

"Not me. I don't want to be a burden on my family." Esther took a sip of her coffee.

"Think of it as payback for all of those meals you cooked for them."

"No, that's not me. What do you know about it anyway?"

"Because I experienced a stroke ten years ago."

"Really. You don't appear to be affected by it." Phyllis was younger than Esther. There was nothing to give her away as a stroke survivor. Esther had thought she was just another nurse or health care professional telling others what to do.

"That's because you didn't know me before the stroke. I had to learn a new normal. Now it's just normal. I've had to let go of a lot of expectations I had placed on myself, had to let my family pick up those things I could no longer do. It was hard, but it's okay. I don't worry half as much as I used to. I guess that was a positive side effect of my stroke. Heck, I don't remember things like I used to, but then I don't remember what I don't remember." She laughed before continuing. "I started by coming as a participant to the group, kept coming back, and eventually I was asked to lead the group."

"I didn't know."

"Sorry. At the start of every new group I give my background. You came in after the group had already been going for a few months. But enough about me. What about you? It's up to you. How do you want to live these years?"

"Not like this."

"Focus on what you still have instead of what you have lost. You have a husband who won't desert you during hard times. Not everyone can say that." She nodded at Peter who had just walked into the room and was scanning it to find Esther. He smiled when he saw her and headed over.

"Ready to go?" Peter asked.

"Yes, I am," Esther responded, setting down her coffee and grabbing her cane with one hand, his arm with the other.

"See you on Friday," Phyllis said. Esther smiled and nodded her assent.

"What were you and Phyllis talking about when I came in?"

"You." Esther smiled.

"Oh really."

"It's all we ever talk about."

"Ha, ha. Tell me, what were you really talking about?" Peter escorted her out to the parking lot.

"We were talking about a new normal. What that would look like."

"What would it look like?" Peter asked as he opened the car door and helped her in.

"I don't know just yet. I want everything to be the way it was."

136

"You know that's not possible." Peter shut the door and went to the driver's side.

"No, I don't know that," she continued the conversation. "Why can't I go back to the way it was?"

"Because it's different now. You can't do everything you used to do."

Esther sighed and stared out the window.

"When Dale died, I had to go on. I had the kids. What else could I do?" Esther paused. "I just wish I could go back to a time when life was easier."

"Has it ever been easy?"

"No, I guess not. Every time has its challenges. I didn't say easy, just easier."

"Maybe this time can be easier, if we make it that way."

"What do you mean?"

"I mean, fighting change just makes it harder. It would be easier if you accepted some help —"

"— Like I have a choice."

"— Let me finish. Yes, you have had to accept help, but you've done it begrudgingly. Accept the help being offered to you. Let go of some of the workload. Let us, me and your family, make things easier for you. Can you do that?"

"I don't know, Peter. I can't be someone I'm not." Esther stared out the window at the rows of houses passing by.

"I'm not asking that. No one's asking that. But maybe you can let up on yourself a little. Learn to accept you can't do everything you used to, then do what you can."

"You mean, accept the new normal?"

"Yes, if you can."

"I don't know if I can do that." Esther continued to stare out the window till they reached home.

Chapter 34

Ashley was a natural at lyrical dance, as Chloe knew she would be. She appeared to enjoy the freedom of expression that the form allowed, though Chloe could tell she didn't want to admit it.

"How do you like it?" Chloe asked her.

"It's okay."

"You seemed to be enjoying yourself."

"I said it was okay." Chloe didn't say anything more.

And it was great having Letty around, catching up on the New York dance scene.

"Who are the girls watching the class?" Letty asked her after the first night of classes.

"That's Grace, Joy's daughter, and her friend Josie."

"Grace? I didn't recognize her. She's grown so. Why aren't they dancing?"

"I put an age restriction on the class, twelve and up. Josie doesn't take any classes. She has something wrong, has difficulty with her feet. Some neurological disorder. I don't know exactly what. I've invited her to join Grace's class just to try it but she always refuses. Grace is taking jazz classes. She doesn't have Ashley's ability. Why?"

"Just wondering. I hate to see anyone sitting out. Must be hard for Grace, living in Ashley's shadow."

"Grace is her own person. No doubt about that. She is as different from Ashley as hip-hop to ballet. She dances for the fun of it. Ashley is the competitor, especially against herself."

Letty had proceeded with the first morning class. During break she went over to talk to Grace and Josie.

"Why aren't you dancing?" she asked.

"We aren't old enough," Grace answered.

"No one sits out during my dance classes. Why don't you join us?"

"You mean it?" Grace jumped up. Josie huddled on the floor as if trying to disappear into the linoleum.

"I can't," she said.

"Can't or won't? There's no room for can't in my class. If you aren't able to do the steps the rest of the class is doing, then do the steps you can."

"No, I can't. You tell her, Grace," Josie pleaded with her friend to rescue her.

"She's right. Her feet don't always work the way they are supposed to. I'll stay with her." Grace sat back down.

"No, you don't. Stand up, both of you. If your feet don't move, then move your arms, move with the music." Letty pulled Josie up from the floor. "You don't have to do the same steps as everyone else to dance. Not in my class. Do the steps you can. Dance to the music in your head." Josie glanced over at Grace, unsure what to do. Grace nodded at her, encouraging her.

"It's okay, Josie. Just move to the music in your head, like she says," Grace told her and swayed back and forth to an imaginary beat. Josie tried, then lost her balance.

"I guess I'm not even good at swaying," she said.

"You are just getting started. Here, hang onto this bar." Letty took her to the rail. "Hold on, now sway, move your arms up and down, gracefully. What is the music in your head?"

"In my head I'm a fairy princess, dancing to elfin music, riding on a unicorn."

"Then move like a fairy princess." Letty helped her raise and lower her arms in a flying motion. "If you think you might lose your balance, then grab on with both hands. If you feel strong enough, then move your feet. How's that?"

"Wonderful," Josie said until she saw the other girls coming back in from break. She stopped.

"Don't pay any attention to them. You dance your own dance. Dance is for everyone. Did you know there are some intergenerational dance groups? Each age group does what they can. The older members move slowly, waving their arms, while the younger members dance around them. Those who can't stand, sit in chairs. Everybody dances."

"My grandma could dance in her wheel chair," Grace said.

"Yes, she could."

"And my grandmother could dance — even with braces?" Josie asked.

"Of course. If you have to sit, that's okay. But everybody dances, everyone moves to the music. Got it?"

"Sure," Grace answered for both of them.

"I've got to get back to the rest of the group. We'll do more over lunch," Letty told them.

Chloe had been watching and listening from the doorway. She was assisting Letty with the class. It helped her further her skills so she could eventually teach the class herself. At lunch she asked Letty about the intergenerational dance group.

"Do you think we could do something like that here? How difficult would it be to put it together?"

"Not hard. I've thought, when I stop dancing professionally, I'd love to have a dance studio where I can offer dance for all students at all levels, including an intergenerational dance group."

"There's always a place for you here," Chloe said.

"Who said I was stepping down yet?"

"When you do, don't forget us."

Letty smiled and took a bite of salad. "I could never forget you, or Joy's School of Dance."

"And I won't let you," Chloe said, her brain working on possibilities.

For the close of the class, Letty assigned the girls to come up with a dance. She didn't assign any particular music or theme. She wanted to see what they would come up with on their own. They had to choreograph their own routine. They had the option of doing it with a group or solo. She wanted to see how much they had learned. In their regular classes the instructors choreographed numbers for the students. The class was going to do a choreographed number for the recital in June, but this was different. It gave the girls the freedom to pick the music and dance style. Letty hadn't tried this with a dance class before. She wanted to see how it would work. The students were welcome to invite their friends and families to see the final product. Some were excited by the challenge, others terrified.

We can't choreograph my own dance, they told Chloe.

"Yes, you can. That's why I restricted this class to the older, more experienced students. You've been dancing long enough. You can do it," Chloe told them. "It'll be fun."

"Chloe," Grace approached her. "Do you think Josie and I can do a dance together? I know we aren't really part of the class …"

"Why, Grace, of course you can do a number. This isn't a competition. Invite your family. Tell Josie to invite her family as well." Everybody dances, Chloe thought. A place for everyone.

Ashley didn't know what kind of dance routine she wanted to do. She was annoyed with the assignment, didn't want to do it. It was taking more time away from her music than she wanted. She liked the class, but then Letty kept picking on her.

"Ashley, you're holding back. This isn't classical ballet. Let your feelings flow through your body. You are telling a story. Not so stiff. Fluid, fluid," she demanded, embarrassing Ashley. Letty was never that tough on the other dancers.

"Why is Letty picking on me?" she complained to Chloe. "I'm better than everyone else, but nothing I do is good enough."

"Maybe because you are better than the other dancers, Letty expects, demands more from you."

"That's not fair"

"I think you should talk to Letty about this, not me."

When she complained to her Aunt Kathleen about the assignment, Aunt Kathleen didn't back her up the way Ashley expected her to.

"Maybe you need to talk to Letty about this," she said.

When she talked to Letty, Letty told her, "Ashley, don't waste my time. Either you are serious about dance or you're not. If you're not, I have other students who are eager to learn."

"What are you talking about? I'm better than Lindsay and Jessica and Janet. You don't treat them the way you treat me. You're all encouraging and praise when they dance. You're even nicer to Grace and Josie than me."

"Ashley, think about it. Why am I easier on them?" Letty paused. Ashley rolled her eyes and looked away. "Because they are doing the best that they can. That is all anyone can ask of a person. You're right. The other girls don't have a tenth of your talent, but what ability they have, they are using. You, on the other hand, are sliding by. You aren't giving this your full effort. I accepted that when you were younger, but not anymore. If you want to just slide by, put together a dance with little effort, you'll still get applause from the people who come, but not from me, because I know what you are capable of. I know you can do so much better. Live up to your mother's blood that beats inside you. She never accepted anything less than her best. Whatever she did, she gave it her all. I expect nothing less from you. If not, then get out of here because you are wasting my time."

Ashley didn't know what to say. What could she say? She'll show her. She'll show Letty and Chloe and Aunt Kathleen. She'll blow them away with her routine. But first, she had to figure out what to do.

"Ashley, look to your heart," Letty had told her before, before she had given up on her. "Look inside. Dig deep. Find your voice," Letty had told her.

"Look to your heart," she heard her mother's voice from deep within. But she was holding back. She didn't want to look to her heart.

Chapter 35

"Since when did you take up jogging?" Julia asked when Kathleen joined her on her morning run. "And, for that matter, since when did you stop drinking? I saw the way you nursed your wine last night, pretending to drink. You aren't fooling me. Are you pregnant?"

"No, just trying to be."

"You are?" Julia stopped running and hugged her. Kathleen squirmed out of her grasp. "That's awesome. Dibs on being godmother. I'll make an amazing godmother."

"I'm sure you would, but I'm not pregnant yet, just trying to be. I read that if you are even thinking about getting pregnant, you should stop drinking. Any amount of alcohol is bad for a developing fetus, even one only a few days old."

"I've heard that too, but think about it. All of those women who become pregnant without planning for it. Do you think all of them stopped drinking? Did you not drink before you knew you were pregnant with Josh and Scott?"

"No. But that was then, this is now. I want to do everything right this time."

"And what about jogging?" Julia started jogging again with Kathleen at her side.

"I read that taking steps to improve your health can improve your chance of getting pregnant."

"Yes, but too much exercise can harm your chances."

"What?" Kathleen stopped, causing Julia to stop and jog in place. "You mean I got up early all for nothing?"

"Not necessarily. It's still good for you. Just don't overdo it. Come on." Julia started running again, leaving Kathleen to trail behind.

"I just want to do everything possible to improve our chances of getting pregnant," Kathleen said when she caught up with Julia, the cold air ripping through her lungs as she spoke.

"Kathleen, just relax, be yourself. Yes, it's good to take certain steps, but, I'm sure you've heard about all of those couples who got pregnant precisely when they had given up."

"Yes, I have, but they weren't as old as I am."

"Maybe not. Still it won't help if you stress out too much about this. Relax. Sometimes God likes to remind us he's still in charge."

"Right." Kathleen struggled to keep up with Julia, too out of breath to continue the conversation. She was happy when she reached the corner where she needed to turn and go on by herself, leaving Julia to run by herself. She quickly slowed down to a trot, then a walk.

Ever since she had started thinking about a baby, each month that passed without a period gave her hope that maybe that miracle would happen, only to leave her disappointed when her period returned. She would get her hopes up, think that maybe because she had placed it all in God's hands, God was going to give her what she so desperately wanted. Was that trying to manipulate God? Doesn't God want for us what is best for us? And who knows better than her what is best for her? God, of course. If only God would see it her way.

The tests from the specialist had come back pretty much how she had expected. Nothing wrong on Joe's part. It was all her. Her eggs were old. The doctor said the chances of her being able to conceive normally with her own eggs were under two percent.

"What do you suggest then, doctor?" Joe had asked.

"I would recommend in vitro fertilization using donor eggs."

"What? Using someone else's eggs? No, I'm not doing that," Kathleen blurted out. "There's no possibility of me getting pregnant using my own eggs?"

"I didn't say that. There is the possibility but not only do you have fewer eggs, the chances of abnormalities, the chances of miscarriage, are greater with old eggs."

"Isn't there anything else we can do?" Joe asked.

"I can put you on hormones to increase the possibility of getting pregnant, but we are still dealing with old eggs."

"Then do that. We can try that, right Joe?"

"Kathleen, let's talk about this."

"What's there to talk about? We already talked about this. We said we would try the fertility drugs."

"But that was before we knew the risk of problems with the pregnancy. Kathleen, we need to talk," Joe told her.

Kathleen cried the whole drive home. When Joe tried to talk to her, she told him to let her cry. She needed to cry. "You don't have to explain it to me. I heard what the doctor said. Just give me some time to take it all in. Then I'll be okay. Just give me this, Joe. Let me cry."

"Are you sure you're okay."

"No, but I will be." I will be, she repeated to herself. Maybe if she repeated it enough it would be true.

Chapter 36

Esther hadn't missed Christmas, all the decorations and preparations. It wasn't just her stroke. Something had shifted inside of her. She just didn't want to work so hard any more. Was she just lazy? Was it a temporary setback or was this the new normal? She surprised herself when she heard her voice saying to Peter, "Do you think it's time we got rid of this house?"

"What are you saying?" Peter put down the paper he was reading and stared over his reading glasses at her.

"This house. Don't you think it's too big for us?"

"It is big." Esther could tell Peter was being careful about what he said. He had brought up this topic before only to be shut down. But she hadn't been ready back then. Now she was.

"Too big, too much work for us."

"Are you sure? Don't you think you should wait a while, wait till you are more yourself?"

"Maybe I am myself, finally. Maybe I'm tired of this house and all of its memories. Maybe I'm ready to move on."

"Honey, you know my thoughts on this subject. But it's your house, your memories. This isn't a decision for me to make."

"Good, then I've decided. Let's look at other places."

"What other places?"

"Retirement communities."

"Who's looking at retirement communities?" They had not noticed Esther's dad coming into the room. "You're not putting me out to pasture."

"No, Dad. Not at all. Peter and I, we are talking about maybe moving out of this house. It's too big for us. I can't keep it up."

"And what about me? Where were you planning on shipping me off to?"

"No plans at all, Dad. Just talking. We wouldn't do anything without consulting you."

"Are you selling this house?" her father continued to question her.

"Haven't got that far. I guess we would have to make it a package deal. You come with the house." Esther could tell her dad didn't appreciate her attempt at humor.

"Ha, ha," her dad said then walked away.

Esther looked at Peter and sighed. Oops.

Chapter 37

Grace and Josie were excited about the assignment. Josie never thought she would ever be able participate in a dance recital. They kept talking about it while Ava drove them home. How annoying, Ashley thought as they prattled on.

"It's not a recital," Ashley stated, "Just some routines at the end of class. There's not going to be any costumes or special lighting or ticket sales. It will be lame."

"Don't listen to Ashley," Ava told Grace and Josie. "I can't wait to see what you do."

Ashley headed upstairs to her attic bedroom and plucked notes on her guitar. Her phone rang. A text from Caleb. "Emergency practice. Tomorrow afternoon. Can you make it?"

Tomorrow was Sunday. They had church and Sunday dinner. She would find a way.

"Sure," she texted back.

Caleb waited for all four band members to gather before dropping his bombshell. He paused for effect, "America's Got Talent is holding auditions in Detroit."

"So?" Ashley said.

"So, I signed us up for an audition."

"You're crazy. We aren't ready for that," Ashley pushed back.

"Maybe you're not, but I am. If you aren't up for it, I can find another guitar player."

"I'm up for it. It's you I'm talking about. You don't want to embarrass yourself, do you?"

"Hey you two, what about the rest of us?" Jesse interrupted. "There are four members to this band."

"Oh, yeah, sorry," Caleb said, still snarling at Ashley. "What do you think?"

"I'm in," Kara, their drummer, said.

"Go for it," Jesse, the bass player, agreed.

"Okay, it's settled. It means we are going to have to double-down on rehearsals."

"Oh?" Ashley said.

"That a problem for you, blondie?"

"No, I'll do it," just how she didn't know. She had ballet twice a week and the classes where she was assisting and now this assignment, and, by the way, school work, but hey, she could do it.

"Good. Let's get to work."

Ashley told her parents about the audition that night.

"Ashley, how are you going to find time to do that?" her dad asked.

"I can do it, Dad. I'll work extra hard."

"But there's your dance classes too. And the assignment and homework," Ava added.

"Then I'll quit ballet if I have to."

"We're not asking you to do that," her dad said.

"I never get to do anything I want," Ashley started.

"Don't you take that tone of voice with us," her dad said.

"This is the opportunity of a lifetime. How can you say no?"

"We didn't say no. We just asked you how you were going to find the time to do it," Ava said.

"I hate you both. Mom would have let me." Ashley stomped out.

Ashley always played the Mom card when she didn't get her way. She knew her dad saw through it, but sometimes it worked on Ava.

"Give her time to cool off," Dale said after she left. "She's playing us, you know, playing the Mom card. Her mother never would have put up with this behavior. Ashley knows that. She thinks she can play you."

"I know that, but maybe she's right. Maybe it is a chance of a lifetime. Or a chance for a life lesson. I just don't know how she can keep up with her classes."

"So, we let her on the condition that her grades don't slide."

"Sounds reasonable to me," Ava agreed.

Reasonable, Dale thought. Was anything reasonable where Ashley was concerned?

Chapter 38

Kathleen surprised Julia when she joined her again for her morning jog.

"I thought you had sworn off exercise," Julia quipped. Kathleen didn't respond with a retort. She wiped away the tears that were running down the side of her checks.

"Kathleen?" Julia stopped running and reached over and grabbed Kathleen. "What's wrong?"

"Everything."

"Tell.me. What did the specialist say?"

"I'm old." Kathleen choked back tears, unable to say more.

"Let's get coffee. We can't talk here." Julia started for a local coffee place.

"And have the whole town gossiping about why the pastor's wife was crying?"

"Better than wondering why she was crying out on the city streets. Come on. We're going to my place." Julia changed course and led Kathleen back in the direction she had come from. When they arrived at the split-level ranch house Julia called home, Julia sat Kathleen down in her breakfast nook while she made a cup of dark roast with her Keurig.

"Is Alex here?" Kathleen asked.

"She won't be up for an hour or more. It's just us," Julia assured her as she put on a tea kettle on the stove.

"No coffee?"

"I've already had my quotient."

"Really? I didn't know that was a thing. Thought you downed buckets of coffee at work." Kathleen wiped her eyes.

"I like to change things up sometimes." Julia set a tea cup at her place. "You ought to try it," she suggested as she sat down across from Kathleen. "Now talk. Tell me what happened."

"I told you. I'm old."

"Other women your age have had babies."

"Other women aren't me."

"Exactly what did the doctor say?"

"He said my eggs were old and that even if I were to get pregnant, the likelihood of a defective fetus resulting in a miscarriage or a baby with serious health issues was great. If we were to try artificial insemination, he wanted to use a donor egg, not my own."

Julia got up to answer the call of the tea kettle, poured the hot water into a pot with tea bags and carried it to the table.

"Those specialists. Sometimes I think they are like surgeons. The only answer to every problem is surgery. They like to use what they have learned, try out all the latest technologies."

"No, I don't think that is the case. I think he's just looking out for our best interest. Why spend all of that money and effort on invitro fertilization if there is such a risk of an abnormality? Besides, invitro fertilization — I hate that term. Sounds like a test-tube baby."

"It kind of is."

"Well. I don't want that."

"What are you going to do? What about hormones?"

"And increase the chance of an abnormal baby? No. Joe and I talked about it. I guess we'll just leave it in God's hands." God's hands — what did that mean? She clasped her hands tightly under the table.

"There are change-of-life babies."

"I know it does happen." Kathleen started to sniff again, still clutching her hands into fists.

"What, Kathleen? Tell me."

Kathleen looked over at her friend, tears swimming in her eyes, overflowing at the corners. She unclasped her hand in order to wrap them around her coffee mug.

"Is it possible to grieve over the loss of a dream you didn't even know you had?"

Julia reached for Kathleen's hand. "Of course, it's possible. Is that what this is about?"

"I never thought I wanted kids. Didn't really want the ones I had at the time I had them, though now I don't know what I would do without them. But the idea of having another baby never occurred to me. It wasn't part of the plan."

"Until it was."

"Yes, until now. And now that I can't have it …"

"It's not impossible."

"— Might as well be. Sometimes time runs out on our dreams, even ones we didn't even know we had."

"What about Joe?"

"He's okay with it. He's more concerned about me. After all, he raised his girls, unlike me. I wasted all those years and now it's too late."

"Yes, it is too late to go back and redo those years, but you can go forward."

"That's what I've been trying to do. I guess that's all I can do." Kathleen shook her head and took a sip of coffee. But is it enough? Will it ever be enough?

Chapter 39

Ashley still had no idea what dance routine to do for her lyrical dance class. She couldn't do something from previous recitals. Chloe would know, as would pretty much everybody else there.

"Why don't you dance to one of your mom's favorite songs?" Aunt Kathleen had suggested.

"This song needs to have words. It has to tell a story. All Mom liked was classical music."

"No, there was other music. Hymns, popular songs. She loved that song, 'I Can Only Imagine.' She played it over and over before she died. Maybe you could dance to that."

Ashley remembered the song, remembered hearing it over and over and over again. She hated it. It reminded her too much of her mom, her last days. No way she would dance to that. But if not that song, which one?

Ashley was up in her room, plucking on her guitar, trying to figure out what to do when she heard Grace call her.

"Not now, Grace. I'm busy."

"Ashley," Grace pounded on the attic door. "Ashley, it's Lucky. Something's wrong. Help us."

Ashley put her guitar aside and climbed down the stairs. "Where is he?"

"He's outside, under the back porch."

Ashley remembered hiding Lucky, first in the shed, then under the porch, when she had first found him. Or when he first found her. That was so long ago, back when her mother was still alive. He had been her dog then. Grace had been a baby.

Jacob was waiting for them. "Where's Dad and Ava?" Ashley asked as she came down the stairs.

"Dad's still at work. Ava had a meeting at school."

Lucky was laying under the porch, refusing to move. When she called his name, his eyes opened, but just for a moment.

"What happened? Is he hurt?" Ashley asked.

"I don't think so. He just crawled in there and won't come out, not even for a treat," Jacob said.

"We better call the vet."

"I'll call Josie. She'll get her mom," Grace said.

"Jacob, you call Dad." Ashley crawled down next to Lucky. When he didn't come out, she crawled under the porch and put his head in her lap.

"It's going to be okay," she told him, reassuring herself.

"Josie's mom is on her way." Grace leaned under the porch. "Do you want me to get anything?"

"Get his blanket. You know, his favorite one." Grace ran upstairs to get Lucky's blanket out of her room where he slept each night.

"How long has he been like this?" Ashley asked Grace when she came back with the blanket.

"He's been hurting for some time. Could hardly make it upstairs any more. But this is the first time he wouldn't eat and wouldn't come in."

How could he have gotten so bad and she not know? How could he have gotten so old? Ashley remembered how he had slept with her when her mom had been so sick. How he had stayed with her after she died. She remembered Howard, Lucky's first owner who had become a member of the family before he died too.

"Lucky, you can't die. You have to stay alive. I'll take care of you, Lucky. Just stay alive," Ashley whispered.

"Every living thing dies. That's what Josie's grandmother says," Grace told her.

"And what does she know?"

"A lot. She's a vet. She said it was only a matter of time till it would be Lucky's turn to die."

Ashley did not want to hear that.

Ashley directed Jacob to wait out front for Josie's mom to get there. "Send her back here as soon as she gets here."

Ashley continued to rub Lucky's ears as she waited. What was taking so long? Grace slid in next to her under the musty porch. Ashley didn't send her away or say anything to her. What was there to say? She breathed in the dampness, then buried her head in Lucky's neck. He smelled like death. Ashley knew the smell. She didn't want to admit it.

"Hang on, Lucky. The vet will be here soon," she whispered.

Jacob came back with the vet and their dad.

"Where is he?" Ashley heard their dad ask Jacob.

"Under the porch." Their dad's face appeared under the porch where the two girls huddled with Lucky.

"Are you two okay?" he asked.

"We're fine, Daddy. Just help Lucky," Ashley answered him.

Grace slid out to give Josie's mom room to crawl under the porch with Ashley and Lucky. She examined him as best as she could in the tight confines.

"He's going to be okay, isn't he?" Ashley asked.

"I'm sorry," she slid far enough out from under the porch so all could hear. "Dogs do this when their time is near. I could take him to the animal hospital, feed him intravenously — but it would only prolong the inevitable. Right now, he is comfortable. He will pass away in his sleep. Or I could give him a shot."

"Don't put him to sleep, Daddy," Ashley said.

"It's just a matter of time, honey," her dad responded.

"That's okay. I want to stay with him."

"You can't stay out here all night," he told Ashley. "Can we move him into the house?" he asked Josie's mom.

"Yes, we can do that without causing him too much pain." Her dad reached in and pulled Lucky off of Ashley's lap and out of the crawl space. He carried him inside and set up a space in the living room where all three kids took turns bringing him water and treats, trying to get him to eat. Ashley didn't resist their help. She was grateful for the company, though she wouldn't tell them. All three laid down alongside of Lucky, never leaving till the next morning. Lucky's eyes, when open, fixed on her. Was he asking her to let him go? She couldn't let him go, until he closed his eyes for the last time and she had no choice.

Ashley watched as her dad wrapped Lucky in his favorite blanket and carried him out of the house.

They buried Lucky under the tree they had planted in memory of their mother.

"Now we have double reason to visit this tree," Jacob said after Pastor Joe said a few words and their dad lifted the last shovel of dirt.

"That we do, Jacob," Dale said as he put his arm around his son and youngest daughter. Ashley stood to the side by herself. When Ava tried to comfort her, she pulled away, walked back to the house and barricaded herself in her room.

Chapter 40

Kathleen was curious to see what the lyrical dance students would come up with, especially Ashley. She had been worried about her after Lucky's death, but Ashley no longer confided in her as she had in the past. Dale said she had locked herself in her attic bedroom. Now and then he thought he heard dance steps. What was that girl up to?

Grace and Josie did a short, bouncy dance that incorporated Josie's unique steps. Her parents and grandmother were delighted. Tears ran down Josie's mother's cheeks as she watched her baby dance. Everyone applauded. Even Jacob was almost complimentary.

"Hey, you didn't suck," he told them. When Josie laughed and stumbled, he reached out and held her up.

Kathleen saw Chloe whisper something to Josie's mother.

"We'll talk after," Chloe said as the next dance started.

"What was that about?" Kathleen leaned in to ask her.

"I told her we might be starting a new dance class, an intergenerational dance class, one Josie might want to be part of. She seemed interested." Kathleen choked back a laugh so as not to interfere with the dance routine taking place.

Then Ashley danced for the class, for her family, all those gathered, and for her mother, to the song, "I Can Only Imagine." Those who remembered Joy were in tears as she danced. Even some who didn't remember her found tears forming.

"Now that's what I've been talking about," Letty told her when she finished. "You didn't hold back." Ashley wiped away her tears as others came up and hugged her.

"That was beautiful," her grandmother said, reaching up from her chair to hug her. "I saw your mother as you danced," Kathleen heard her whisper into Ashley's ear.

"I thought you hated that song," Kathleen said when she got a chance to talk to Ashley.

"I know, I did, but I couldn't get it out of my head. I saw my mom dancing to it. Finally, I had to dance, too." Ashley eyes started to tear up again. "It was for my mom."

Kathleen wiped away tears from her own eyes, as Ashley allowed her to give her a hug.

Aunt Kathleen surprised her two days later. "I've got you an audition on America's Got Talent."

"Aunt Kathleen, I already have an audition, with my band."

"Oh, that. Don't worry. This is just you. You're going to dance just like you did on Saturday."

"I don't think they allow you to audition more than once," Ashley said as she put her ballet slippers on for class.

"I've got it all taken care of. You'll be great."

"What if I don't want to audition?"

"Why wouldn't you? Of course, you want to. What girl wouldn't want to?"

"Me." Ashley stood up and stretched.

"You'll be great. Do this just this once. Do it for me."

Ashley agreed but, where Aunt Kathleen was concerned, she knew that wouldn't be the end of it.

The day for the auditions arrived. Ashley rode to Detroit with her Aunt Kathleen and the rest of the family and met up with her band.

"We're playing at ten-twenty," Caleb told her. "You sure you're up for this?"

"What, you looking for an excuse to back out?" Ashley asked.

"No way. I just wanted to make sure you were ready."

"Ready as I'll ever be, right group?" Ashley looked at the rest of the band. Kara's face was ashen. "Don't worry, Kara. You'll be great. We'll be great. And even if we aren't, we can have fun."

"Right," Caleb agreed. "Let's get out there and have some fun."

Their band played a variety of grunge music, loud being the main component. Ashley and Caleb faced off, singing back and forth at each other, bouncing up and down and tossing their hair.

"This is what they've been practicing all these years?" Kathleen commented to Dale and Ava as they watched from the side of the stage.

"I guess so," Dale said.

"I don't remember it being so loud when they practiced in our garage," Ava said.

Jacob bounced along with the band, dancing and playing air guitar. Kathleen was surprised when the judges didn't buzz them, bringing this misery to an end.

Ashley and Caleb were clearly having fun, smiling and singing back and forth at each other. They bowed deeply at the end and waited with grins for applause. Jacob and Grace cheered. Other family members of the band clapped.

"Oh boy, here we go," Kathleen said as Simon prepared to speak.

"How long have you been playing together? It says here, three years?" Simon asked.

"Yes, that's right," Caleb answered.

"Well, I must say, you just don't have it. I don't think any number of years of practice will get you there. I vote no."

"You looked like you were having fun," Howie said. "Keep playing and having fun. But don't plan on making it a career." Another no. Four no's. They walked off stage as family members helped them move their instruments.

"Maybe this will put an end to all of this nonsense," Kathleen heard Caleb's dad comment to Dale.

"You were great," Jacob told Ashley.

"Simon didn't think so," Ashley responded.

"What does Simon know anyway?" Kathleen said as she hugged Ashley. "We've got to get you ready for your dance number."

"I don't think I can do it, Aunt Kathleen. I can't go back out there."

"Remember, you promised."

"I know, but …"

"No buts. You'll be great. Just focus on the music."

Ashley slid out of her grunge and let Ava fix her hair. On the stage Kathleen heard Simon comment, "Not another grunge band."

"No, the next audition is a dancer. Ashley Reese."

"That's you, Ashley," Kathleen kissed her on her forehead. "Do this for me. Or if not for me, do it for your mom. Dance for your mom."

Ashley took a deep breath, walked out on stage and posed as she waited for the beginning notes. Kathleen watched as Ashley set aside her disappointment in order to focus on the words of the song. She was a true professional. She could only imagine. Kathleen could only imagine what it would be like to see Ashley's mom again. She was seeing her in Ashley's slight frame, her poise, her grace. The dance began.

The applause this time was real. Two of the judges even stood up. Simon was the first to respond.

"Ashley. It says here you've been dancing since you were three."

"Yes, sir."

"And your mother was a dancer too. She died when you were seven. You dedicated your dance to her?"

"I just dance. I didn't write any of that."

"Then who did?"

"My Aunt Kathleen, I guess."

"Is Aunt Kathleen here today?"

"Yes, she's over there?" Ashley pointed off the stage to where Aunt Kathleen waited in the wings. Kathleen did a slight hand wave in Simon's direction.

"Aunt Kathleen, come on out," Simon said.

Kathleen looked about her, searching for an escape.

"Go on, Kathleen," Dale pushed her forward. She slid up next to Ashley, unsure where to stand, what to do with her hands. If only she had Ashley's poise and grace. If only she had taken dance lessons when she was young. She smiled awkwardly at the judges, waiting to hear not just Ashley's fate, but her fate.

"You must be very proud of your niece," Simon said.

"Very," Kathleen responded.

"It says here, Ashley, all you want to do is dance. Is that correct?" Simon continued.

"No. Aunt Kathleen wrote that. I'm a musician. I write songs and play guitar."

"Didn't we see you two acts earlier in a band?"

"Yes. That's my band."

"You managed to get two auditions?"

"That was me," Kathleen stepped forward. "Ashley didn't have anything to do with it. I entered her. It's okay, isn't it?"

Simon paused for a moment before responding.

"Your aunt did you a favor, Ashley, because that band is going nowhere. If you want to make it to Hollywood someday, dance is your talent, not music. You show a lot of potential, a lot of feeling. Your mother would be proud of you. With enough practice you could make it. I vote no. Forget about guitar and come back in another year or two and show us what you can do."

Ashley had one yes vote, but the others were no's, with directions to come back in a year.

"I'd say, yes, but I don't think you are ready yet," Heidi said. "I'd love to see you again when you've had more time to mature as a dancer."

Everyone hugged Ashley when she came back stage except Kathleen. Ashley refused to let her. Instead she pouted.

"What's wrong? They liked your dance and said to come back," Ava said. "That's better than a lot of acts."

"Simon said our band was no good."

"Hey, being criticized by Simon is a plus. Lots of people wait in line just to hear him put them down. No big deal," Kathleen said. "The important thing is that he liked your dance routine."

"And what you said about my mom. Why did you say that?" Ashley glared at her aunt.

"It's what the judges are looking for. It has audience appeal. Everyone roots for the girl whose mother is gone. I didn't think you would mind. It's true."

"Yes, but I don't want to use that to get on any show. I want to do it on my own merit."

"And you will someday," Dale told her and put his arm around her. "Now get changed and we'll get ice cream."

Kathleen trailed along behind Dale and Ashley as they walked out. Not how she had thought this morning would end.

Chapter 41

Esther waited for Peter to put down his cell phone. "That was Kathleen. She says Ashley did great with her dance routine."

"Is she going to Hollywood?" Esther asked.

"No, but the judges want her to come back, said she wasn't ready for Hollywood just yet. So that's good."

"What about the band?"

"The judges hated them. Said they were going nowhere."

"Poor Ashley."

"Why? She got great reviews on her dancing."

"But what she loves is her music. It's hard to be told you're no good at what you love to do." Esther sighed. Didn't she know the truth of that.

"Is it? Or is it better to hear it now before you spend your life on it. Now she can play for the fun of it."

"Still, it's hard to accept your limits."

"Are we talking about Ashley or you?" Peter asked. Esther chose to ignore the comment.

"High school years are hard." Esther shook her head as she remembered her own years in high school, so long ago.

"You don't have to tell me. I was a probation officer working juvie once, remember."

"Peter, I can hardly remember what I did. How can I remember what you did? I remember those early years better than the later years."

"That's why you have me to help you remember."

Esther turned away from him with a sigh as memories came back unbidden. "Were you drafted for the Vietnam War?" She stared ahead as she asked.

"No. I wasn't drafted. I tried to sign up but they wouldn't have me. My eye sight was too bad. I was 4F. Guess it was a good thing. I doubt I would have been much good at it. Why do you ask?"

"I remember one of my friends, her brother came back from the war. He was never the same after that. Sat in the dark watching TV. One day he just left. Didn't tell anyone where he was going. He went out West and walked in front of a train, like thousands of other Vietnam vets."

"Those were hard times."

"Yes, they were." Yes, they were, Esther repeated to herself.

Esther didn't know what she would have done after Bobby's death if not for Dale. Dale helped her navigate those early days of grief, diverted her attention with his joking manner and teasing. When it was his turn to face the draft, she had panicked. One of her friends' brother had died over there. Another had come back as good as dead. He never talked about what had happened. Didn't talk about anything. Sat and stared at the TV screen.

"I don't know what I would do if anything happened to you. What are you going to do if your number comes up?" she asked Dale.

"I'll go. What else can I do?" Dale shrugged his shoulders.

"Some people go to Canada."

"Cowards. I wouldn't do that."

"It's not cowardly if you are doing it out of your beliefs. Then it's a courageous act of resistance." Esther willed him to agree with her. It didn't work. It never worked, but she tried anyway. She never could get Dale to do something he didn't want to do, or not do something he wanted to do.

"I still call them cowards."

Dale's number came up, not in the first third, or the first half, but not in the last third of the numbers where he would have been safe. He was just off of the middle where it was still possible for him to be drafted. Esther had prayed and worried until the year was up and he

165

hadn't been called to serve. She breathed a sigh of relief until Dale suggested he might enlist.

"Why would you do that?"

"To serve my country. What else?"

"But what about me?"

"Would you wait for me?" Dale smiled and put his arms around her.

"Would there be someone to wait for? You know about the body bags." Esther pushed him away.

"Well, I haven't decided yet. Just thinking."

Dale could be infuriating like that. She didn't know whether he was serious or just teasing her to see what she would say. He was a risk taker, unlike her. She kept her feet firmly on the ground. Why take chances? It came as no surprise when he was hired by the electric company out of high school and trained to be a line man. He loved climbing those poles and waving down at her. She had refused to watch.

At least he hadn't been drafted and taken away from her. At least she had had a few good years with him, she told herself.

Chapter 42

"You free?" Caleb texted Ashley.

"Sure," she texted back.

"Can we meet?"

"Where?"

"Park."

"Be there in ten minutes." Ashley jumped off of her bed, put on her shoes, climbed down the ladder to her attic bedroom and ran down the stairs. Ashley didn't know what this was about, but she had her suspicions.

"Going to the park," she yelled to her dad and Ava as she ran out the back door and grabbed her bike.

"Don't be late for dinner," Ava yelled after her.

Ashley rode to the park, to the spot where she had first met Caleb, where she had met the band. She remembered that day, all the hopes for being part of a band. Was it over just because of some stupid TV personality?

Caleb was already there waiting for her. She hopped off her bike, propped it up and sauntered over to Caleb.

"Hey," she said.

"Hey," Caleb replied. "You did good yesterday. Your dance. Even I could tell it was good."

"I didn't get a ticket to Hollywood."

"But you will if you come back."

"If I come back."

"Why wouldn't you? If I had your talent, I would jump on the possibility."

"Well, you aren't me. So, when's our next rehearsal?"

"That's what I wanted to talk about." Caleb turned aside and stared down at his feet.

"You aren't ending the band, are you?"

"Why continue? Besides, my dad says I need to settle down, get a job, save for college."

"You can do that and still play in the band." Ashley stared at him. He kept his head down as if afraid to meet her gaze.

"Why? You heard what Simon said. We're a bunch of no-talent losers." Caleb shuffled his feet as he spoke.

"That's not what he said."

"He might as well have said it. He said we're going nowhere."

"Since when do we listen to what others say?" Ashley could feel anger rising from her stomach through her chest and up to behind her eyes.

"When it's Simon Cowell."

"Well, I'm not listening to him. I plan to continue to play my guitar." She wasn't listening to him, and Caleb shouldn't either. Why couldn't he see that?

"I should have listened to you. We weren't ready." Caleb glanced over at her and shrugged his shoulders.

"No, we were as good as some of those other bands. We just have to work harder."

"You heard him. No amount of practice will make a difference."

"If that's what you want. I just didn't think you would give up so easily." Ashley turned away from him and prepared to leave.

"Hey, we gave it three years. It's been fun. Time to grow up. That's what my dad says."

Ashley turned back around, the anger knot in her stomach softening. "It has been fun, hasn't it? The fun doesn't have to end. We can still play for fun."

"Yeah, but I don't know how much time I'll have. My dad is getting me an after-school job at his business."

"Weekends?" Ashley asked.

"I'll be working weekends too."

"Then I guess the band is history." Ashley was disappointed, but not as disappointed as she had thought she would be.

"Unless you want to take it over." Caleb raised his eyebrows at her, waiting for her response.

"No, that's okay. I guess I knew this would happen someday."

"We can still hang out together, can't we?"

"When? Will you have time?"

"I'll make time." Caleb stared back down at the ground, hands in his coat pockets, and shuffled his feet again. "You want to maybe go to a movie sometime?"

Ashley looked down too. She hadn't quite expected this. "Yeah, sure. When you have time."

"Maybe next Saturday. I get off of work at noon. We could go to a matinee?" He glanced over at Ashley.

"Okay," she agreed. She was surprised by the warm flush of pleasure she felt at the plan.

"Then it's a date." Caleb pulled his hand free of his pocket and extended it to Ashley.

Ashley ignored his hand, reached over and lightly kissed him on the cheek. "It's a date," she said, climbed on her bike and rode away.

Chapter 43

"Kathleen, I have to talk to you. Are you free?" Julia didn't even wait for her to say hello. What was going on?

"We're just finishing breakfast." She glanced across the table at Joe.

"Meet me at the coffee place?"

"I'll be there in fifteen." Kathleen clicked off her phone. "Something's up. I have to meet Julia."

"What is it?"

"I don't know, but it sounded important. You don't mind, do you?"

"Go ahead," Joe said. "I'll take care of the dishes." That's what Kathleen wanted to hear. "After all, you clean up after me when I'm called out on emergencies." Married life is not bad, she thought as she grabbed her purse.

Julia was already sitting at a table far away from the counter when Kathleen arrived. She motioned for Kathleen to join her, pointing to the extra coffee at the table.

"Your favorite," she said.

"What's going on?" Kathleen asked as she sat down.

Julia hushed her then looked around to make sure no one was within ear-shot. "Kathleen, I don't know how to tell you this. I'm so sorry, but I'm pregnant," she stated softly.

"You're what?" Kathleen whispered back. "Does Henry know?"

"I just found out myself. I took the test this morning. I'm sorry. Here you are, wanting a baby and you can't have one, and I don't want a baby but I'm having one. Life just isn't fair." Julia wrapped her hands more tightly around her coffee cup. "What am I going to do? I can't raise another kid."

"Calm down, Julia. Give yourself some time to take it in. Give me some time to take it in." Kathleen took a deep breath before continuing. "How did it happen?"

"Really? Duh." Julia raised her eyebrows and shook her head.

"No, I mean, weren't you being careful? Aren't you on the pill?" Kathleen slid closer to her friend.

"I am, or was, or, I missed a few times."

"A few times? How many is that?"

"I don't know. Who can keep track of such things?" Julia shrugged her shoulders and looked away.

"Apparently not you. You have to tell Henry."

"That's the problem. He'll be ecstatic."

"That's good. What's the problem? He'd marry you in a heartbeat. He's crazy about you." Kathleen didn't understand. If it had been her, she would have been happy, after the initial shock. But she wasn't Julia.

"But what if I don't want to get married?"

"Then you have a problem. Are you ready to do the single parent thing again?"

"No, I don't know." Julia stared down at the coffee that was growing cold in her cup. "What will Alex say? Here I've talked to her about being careful, and I go out and do what I told her not to do."

"I think that's one of your least concerns at this point." Kathleen took a sip of her coffee. "Do you think it's possible that maybe you wanted to get pregnant?"

"What? Are you crazy?" Julia raised her head and stared at Kathleen.

"Think about it. You know how birth control works. You know better than to skip a few days."

"I didn't skip them, I just forgot."

"Yeah, yeah, whatever. Do you think that maybe unconsciously you wanted a baby?" Kathleen continued to push the question.

"But why? Why would I do that?"

"Because you're just as crazy about Henry as he is about you but you're too stubborn to marry him. Maybe this is one way to force the issue." Kathleen took another sip of coffee, allowing her words to sink in.

"If it is, it's a pretty stupid way to do it. How dumb do you think I am?"

"Not dumb, but human. We humans don't always do the smart thing. Sometimes we slip-up. Sometimes we have to be reminded that we aren't always in control. That God may have other plans for us." The words sounded as surprising to her as she was sure they sounded to Julia. Who was she to talk to anyone about God's plans? Yet the words slipped out.

"Is that what you think? That this is somehow part of God's great 'master plan' for me and Henry?"

Kathleen shrugged her shoulders, "Maybe. I think God's plan is for our own good. His plan is for us to be happy, but we resist so sometimes God has to intervene. Or maybe we intervene by not taking our birth control pills."

"You are worse than your husband. If I wanted talk about God, I would have called the priest. This isn't a God thing. It's a human thing."

"Call it what you want. God works through human things." Kathleen smiled before continuing. "And now a human is growing inside of you. What are you going to do about it?"

"I guess I have to tell Henry. But not right now." Julia shook her head and took a sip of her cold coffee. "Should I be drinking coffee?"

"You tell me. You're the doctor."

"And I have patients to see. This can wait."

"But not too long."

"No, not too long, but for now." She finished her coffee but didn't get up. "Kathleen, what am I going to tell Henry? What am I going to do?"

"You'll tell Henry. Together you'll get through this. You aren't alone. You have Henry, and you have me." Kathleen squeezed her friend's hand, giving her encouraging words Joe had given her. Maybe if she said it enough, she would believe it herself.

Chapter 44

"Do you think my mom would want to attend your healing service? It might do her some good," Kathleen asked Joe over their morning coffee.

"Might, but I'm not the one to invite her. In case you haven't noticed, I'm not exactly her favorite person right now."

"She'll get over it."

"Will she? I wonder." Joe and the priest from St. Paul's were putting on a joint healing service that Sunday night. It was something they had been talking about for a while. The new young priest was said to have a gift for healing. Joe had told her about incidents at the hospital when Fr. John prayed over his parishioners. Joe had healing services for his church members. He had talked to her about having an ecumenical service with a healing team composed of various ministers from town. So far, Fr. John was the only one to accept his invitation, but they were going ahead anyway. The Lutheran Church was not that far from the Catholic church in belief and practice. Their services had many common elements. It was natural for them to team up.

Kathleen had mentioned the service to her mom before this and gotten no response either way. She decided to try again, only stronger.

"Mom, I'm going to the healing service at the Catholic church and you are coming with me, no arguments," she announced that afternoon after Sunday dinner. Her mom had not attended church since the stroke.

"I don't want anyone's pity," she insisted. "I'll go when I can walk in on my own two feet," she had said at first, but now that she was walking with a cane, she set a new, higher goal. "I'll go back when I get rid of this cane." Kathleen saw through it. Her mom looked at Peter for help.

"Don't bring me into this. She's your daughter. You deal with her," Peter replied, excusing himself from the discussion. Her mom must have seen the determined expression on Kathleen's face and realized there was no way she was going to back down.

"Okay. What time?"

"Oh," Kathleen had expected more of a fight. "I'll pick you up at six thirty." Kathleen was even more surprised when her mom was ready to go when she came to pick her up.

"Did you have something to do with this?" she took Peter aside to ask.

"No, she decided to go herself, using her own free will." Peter appeared just as surprised as Kathleen as Esther put her coat on and proceeded out the door.

"Wait for me, Mom," Kathleen hurried to help her mom down the steps.

Esther was not on the best terms with God. She was angry with him, but she figured the least she could do was give him a chance or a piece of her mind. She would go to the service and then when nothing happened, maybe Kathleen, maybe everyone, would just leave her alone, let her be.

After Bobby had died, Esther started going to church with Dale. He didn't demand it of her, just offered. She accepted. She needed something to hold onto, something besides Dale. And she found it.

"Mom, why don't you and Dad go to church?" Esther asked one Sunday after coming home from the service. She plopped down on the swing, next to where her mom was seated in a wicker chair.

Her mother closed her eyes and sighed before answering. "Seems I just got angry with God when God destroyed my dreams."

"How did God destroy your dreams?"

"Maybe God didn't. Life happens. But back then, that was how it seemed. I had always wanted a big family. It was all I ever wanted. I married your dad straight out of high school and you came along and I thought I was on my way to having that dream."

"Then what happened?"

"I had two miscarriages. When I made it to five months with Bobby, I was so happy. I thought I had finally beat the curse. My life was back on track."

"I didn't know you had two miscarriages." What else hadn't her mom told her? Esther resisted the urge to scold.

"You didn't? No, I guess you wouldn't. You were so young, just a baby yourself. We didn't talk about such things back then. Still don't that much. You were just supposed to put it behind you, like it wasn't a real baby. But I know they were real babies. I still grieve them."

"What happened when Bobby was born? I know you were sick for a long time."

"I never told you?"

"Tell me now." Esther swung slowly on the swing as she listened to the story unfold.

"It was a hard labor and delivery. The doctor decided I needed a C-section. I was in no shape to argue. You didn't argue with your doctor. You just did what he told you. The placenta had pulled away and I was hemorrhaging. The doctor did what he had to do to save my life. At least that is what he told me. He took away my utcrus and killed my dreams."

"But you would have died."

"I guess so, but he may as well have killed me on that operating table. That was what I thought back then. All those babies I would never have. Grandma told me I needed to live in the present instead of in that imaginary future I had made for myself. Told me to stop grieving over what I would never have and rejoice over what had been given me. It didn't help. I grieved for a long time. I guess that was when I decided to stop going to church. I stopped pretty much everything."

"I remember that. I could tell something was wrong. It was as if you had gone somewhere far away and I couldn't find you." Esther's eyes softened as she remembered those days.

"Was it, Essie? I didn't realize that. I thought you were too little to tell anything."

"But then you came back, though not the same. What brought you back?"

"I don't know. I think I just decided to live. That I was here and I might as well make the best of it."

"That simple?" How could it be so simple? Her life was never that simple.

"It wasn't simple back then. It was a hard choice for me. I guess I made it because here I am."

"But what about God?"

"Oh, God. I blamed him for my losses. Decided to have nothing more to do with him. And then he gave my poor baby cancer. It was retribution for my sins. God should have taken me, not my little Bobby." Her mother started to cry as she always did whenever she mentioned Bobby.

Esther swung back and forth as her mother wiped her tears. What could she say? Was it retribution? That didn't seem like the God she was learning about. She wished Dale were there to help her, help her mom.

"Mom, I don't think God works that way," Esther said as her mother pulled another handkerchief out of her apron pocket.

"Like what?"

"I don't think Bobby's death was retribution for your sins. That makes it all about you. I don't think you're that important. I don't think any of us are that important that God would kill someone to punish us. What would that say about God? Seems unfair to kill someone because of what someone else did." Esther stopped the swing so she could focus on her mother. "And what about Bobby? What did he do to be punished so? All those years of suffering. I don't understand why Bobby had to die, but at least he's not suffering anymore. I don't believe God killed Bobby, I think it just happened. I don't know why you had to suffer the way you did. I don't understand much of any of this, but I don't believe God is responsible." Esther began swinging gently again before continuing.

"Believing in God makes sense to me. In a world where good people like Bobby die, it makes sense. If there is no God, then where is Bobby now? I have to believe. I don't understand, but I have to believe there is more to this life than this."

"And if that works for you, good," her mother stated.

Esther kept going to church with Dale, and one day her mom and dad showed up. Kind of like when her mom decided to rejoin the living, back so many years ago, after Bobby was born.

If the hysterectomy, the miscarriages, Bobby's cancer and the loss of her ability to have children drove her mom away from God, then Bobby's death drove her back to him.

Chapter 45

The service was being held in the Catholic church. Esther had been there before for funerals and weddings. It was more ornate than she was used to, but she liked the stained-glass windows that lined either side of the building, even if they blocked out the sunlight and kept her from gazing outdoors. In the Middle Ages, stained-glass windows told the story of the Bible to peasants who couldn't read the book themselves. The windows also helped blot out the sight of the poverty, destitution and struggle that was their lot in life. The idea was to focus on God inside, not the world outside, or so a priest had told her once. She liked the idea now. Her present reality wasn't exactly a bright one. She wanted an escape from that reality.

Kathleen insisted they sit close to the altar. "This way you can participate without having to walk down the aisle." The first pews were reserved for individuals with limited mobility who wanted to be prayed over.

The service began with music as Fr. John and Pastor Joe came down the aisle together, bowed to the altar, then welcomed everyone and explained how the service would proceed.

There were readings on healing, then a message by Fr. John. Then a deacon and a lay leader joined Fr. John and Joe in the front as part of the prayer team. First, they went to those seated in the front pews.

"What do you want us to pray for?" Fr. John asked her.

"For healing from her stroke," Kathleen told him when she didn't answer right away. Esther was skeptical. What good would it do? Maybe a warm momentary feeling, but no healing. She had been prayed over before. Joe had prayed over her while she was in the hospital. A lot of good that had done. She felt warmth as the members of the prayer team placed their hands on her and Fr. John's words were comforting, but that was all that happened. No miracle.

Joe invited all who wanted prayer to come forward for individual prayer. Esther watched as the pews behind her emptied and people came forward for prayer. Some were older than her, worse off than her. Others were younger. She wondered what they needed healing for. Pew after pew, people came forward to have hands laid on them and prayers said as members of the team took turns praying for each individual. Strains of "Amazing Grace" filled the church, then the choir broke into words about chains being gone, and being set free.

The music filled her whole being, echoing in her soul. She was caught up in the moment. My chains are gone? What did that mean? The chains holding her to this earth, this worldly life, could they finally be broken? In an instant, it was as if the chord that tied her to this life was released and she was in another world, another reality. She saw the people coming forward for prayer, felt their pain, the suffering of the aged, loneliness, heartaches. It was a battle between good and evil and she was caught up in it. Evil in the form of so much human suffering. Good in the healing presence doing battle with that suffering. Then she left that space and seemed to find herself surrounded by clouds. There was Dale, waiting for her.

"Why did you leave me?" she asked him.

"I didn't want to leave you."

"But you did." Then she saw Joy, her daughter-in-law, surrounded by a throng of people dressed in translucent robes of white, all dancing.

"Who are they?" she asked Dale.

"Those are the ones who have been washed in the blood of the Lamb. They have been washed clean through suffering."

"Suffering?" Esther asked. Then she heard a heavenly chorus singing hymns of praise and welcome. Alleluia, they sang as a woman was welcomed and given a crown.

"That's the crown she forged throughout her life," Dale told her.

"She must have been someone special, a martyr or a saint."

"She was. She was a wife, mother and grandmother. Just like you." At this Dale was gone.

Then Esther saw a beautiful crown, laden with gems. In the middle was a stone in a color she had never seen before. It shone with a light that filled the sky and a voice spoke.

"This is the crown you have been creating all your life. The gems are your children, grandchildren, all the people you have loved and helped during your life."

"What is the stone in the middle?" Esther asked.

"That is the greatest gem of all, your stroke."

"My stroke. How can that be a gem? I didn't do anything."

"In your weakness, you allow me to shine through. In your weakness is my strength. Out of your suffering, I'm able to bring good, good you can't see or understand. It is your shining glory. Do you want to throw it away?" What was he talking about? Her mind swirled, trying to understand, but deep inside she understood in a way that surpassed words.

At that, Esther returned to where she was. The choir was still singing, lines continued to flow down the aisle. She thought she had been gone for hours but realized it had been but a moment, if that long.

"Where am I?" Esther whispered to Kathleen.

"In the Catholic church. Is something wrong?"

"You didn't see it? Them?"

"See what?"

"Your dad, Joy, the crown."

"Are you all right, Mom?"

Esther gazed at the crucifix on the wall where Jesus' suffering body was displayed for all to see. "Yes, I'm all right. I'm just fine." The words from Paul swirled in her head, "I consider that the sufferings of this present time are as nothing compared with the glory to be revealed for us." There was meaning in her suffering.

Kathleen had come to the healing service for her mom. She knew it was the only way she would have gotten her mom to attend. She wasn't a big believer in these services. Sure, Jesus healed people, but that was during the age of miracles, when Jesus walked the earth. That time was over.

"Some would say the fact that you are not only attending church but married to a minister is a miracle," that voice in her head told her. Okay, so maybe there are modern-day miracles. She didn't expect to see one that night. But she would try anything to get her mom back, for her to be the person she once was. And if that meant an additional church service, she was okay with that. What she wasn't okay with was being prayed over. When the prayer team asked her what she wanted prayers for, she said, "nothing."

"I'm just here for my mom," she added.

"There must be something you want prayer for," Fr. John said. Kathleen looked at Joe for help. Get her out of this, her eyes said. He shrugged his shoulders. Darn him anyway.

"There's nothing, Father. I'm in good health."

"Then mental healing, guidance?"

The manse appeared in her brain. She hated living there. And whether to have a baby. "No, Father, nothing."

"God knows what you need. We'll pray for that." Fr. John laid his hands on her and started praying. On the outside, Kathleen remained calm, as befitting a minister's wife. Inside she squirmed. What was he doing? How dare he pray for her against her will? Or was it against her will? By coming, sitting in the front row, doesn't that imply consent? And how could she say no to Fr. John? There was something compelling about his presence. Her internal noise was so loud she hardly caught the words of his prayers. Something about inner healing and peace. She couldn't block out the feeling of warmth that was emanating from his hands. Maybe he did have a gift?

"Thank you," she said as he moved on to the next person. Part of her wanted to ask her mom about the experience, the other part rested in the silence. Even when her mom asked her about seeing a crown, it didn't faze her. She didn't know what had happened, but a sense of peace surrounded her. She was okay with her life with the manse — that monstrosity — and whatever God may have in store for her. She didn't know what that was, but she was at peace. She glanced sideways at her mom. What was it her mom had experienced?

They didn't talk on the way home. It just didn't seem right to talk about such things. Each rested in the feelings of the night, holding their experience close.

Chapter 46

"Have I ever told you about my brother, Bobby?" Esther asked as she and Kathleen sat on the back porch, enjoying the early vestiges of spring.

"What? You have a brother? I have an uncle I didn't know about? I would have remembered something like that."

"I guess I didn't," Esther carefully chose her words, not just because of the after effects of the stroke, but because of the content. "It was so long ago. He died when I was sixteen, from leukemia."

"Leukemia. Mom, don't you think this is something I need to know? If for nothing else but my health history, and the kids' health history. This puts us at greater risk for cancer."

"I suppose." Esther wasn't going to let this upset her. She continued to carefully choose her words. "It's funny how these things happen in families. You live a lifetime together and yet you never talk. There are some things you don't bring up, not on purpose. You just don't think about it."

"How can you not think about a brother who died?"

"Oh, I think about him, but so much has happened since then. I guess I never thought to tell you. Didn't think you needed to know. Didn't think you wanted to know."

"Was I that bad in high school?"

"Worse."

"I said I'm sorry before this, haven't I?"

"Funny, I don't remember. Must have lost it with the stroke. Tell me again." Esther smiled and attempted a wink.

"Okay, Mom. I'm sorry for all I put you through in high school and beyond. Is that enough?"

"I don't know that I caught all of that. Could I hear it again?"

"Ha, ha, Mom. How about, thank you for putting up with me and for raising my kids when I wasn't able to? You know, Mom, I can't thank you enough for that."

"That's more like it. Now what were we saying about my brother?"

"No, you never told me you had a brother."

"Looks like it'll be an early spring." Esther gazed out over the yard, enjoying the warm breeze across her face. "Have you thought about having more kids?"

"Mom, what brought that up? Why would I want more kids when the two I have are finally on their own? And Joe's daughters, too. Why would we want to go there?"

"Just wondering. You know I always wanted a big family. Then your father died. That was the end of that dream. Your grandmother, she always wanted a large family, too. All she ended up with was me. Maybe that's why I never told you about Bobby."

"I don't get it, Mom."

High above Esther could see birds sailing through the sky. She stopped and watched them circle and swoop, then glanced down at the slippers on her feet. They looked good there. Sometimes it was nice to let others take care of you.

"Mom, what are you talking about? What does Grandma not having kids have to do with you not telling me about my uncle?"

"You know Grandma."

"Yes, I do, did. She was great."

"That's because you were her granddaughter. It was different being her daughter. She was such a crepe hanger."

"What does that mean?"

"She never let go of anything. Always expected the worse, like hanging black crepe over everything, every event. Is that the right word?"

"What about Bobby?"

"I didn't want to be like her, never letting go of the past, hanging on to the negative. I always tried to live in the present, focus on the positive. That time, Bobby's death, that was a hard time."

"As was Dad's death."

"Yes."

"And my running off."

"Yes."

"And your stroke."

"Yes, maybe that was the hardest of all. I don't know. They were all hard in their own way. Grandma so wanted to have lots of kids. Did you know she had two miscarriages?"

"No, I didn't."

"She continued to grieve for them. She grieved over the children she never had till the day she died. I didn't want to be like that."

In the distance, Esther heard the sound of returning geese, honking on their way to the pond nearby.

"You remember Grandma's big front porch and swing?"

"I loved that swing."

"I did too. Much as I love this house, I always missed having a big front porch and a swing."

"Why didn't you add one on?"

"Couldn't afford it after your father died."

"You could now."

"No, I think I'm getting too old for this house." She gazed out across the lawn, so many good memories, watching her children play in the back yard, and then her grandchildren.

"Are you thinking of selling?"

"No, actually giving it. If you and Joe will have it. I'd like it to stay in the family. So many memories. And I know how you hate living in the manse."

"It's okay. I'm growing accustomed to it."

"Kathleen Marie, don't lie to your mother." A slight laugh escaped her throat as she caught her daughter in a lie.

"Okay. I hate it. But what are you and Peter going to do? And Grandpop?"

"We've put a down payment on one of those condos at that senior living community. Everything on one floor. We have the option of eating in the main dining room if we want, lots of activities and no more maintenance worries. Downsizing. We think it's time. The stairs are just too much for me, even with the chair lift. What we really want to do is travel."

"Wow. So this is happening?"

"Yes, it is. Talk to Joe. See what he thinks."

"And Grandpop?"

"He comes with the house, if that's okay."

"More than okay. It wouldn't be the same without him, just as it won't be the same without you."

"So back to my original question, have you thought about kids? You're not getting any younger, you know. If I can't have all the kids I wanted, maybe I can make up for it with grandkids." She imagined a new generation of children growing up in this house, playing in the yard. Her legacy. "This is a great place for raising kids. You could build that front porch."

"Wait, does this house come with strings attached?"

"No, only hopes and dreams." Esther smiled as she continued to watch birds fly over the yard, swooping and sailing by, landing somewhere in the distance.

Chapter 47

"What would you think about moving into my mom's home?" Kathleen asked Joe over dinner that night.

"We've already talked about this. There's just not enough room."

"There will be when Mom and Peter move out." Kathleen scooped out mashed potatoes and passed them to Joe.

"They're moving?"

"Yes. Mom wanted to know if I … if we wanted the house."

"What do you think?" Joe helped himself to the potatoes.

"I think it's the answer to our prayers," Kathleen said.

"Really. I thought you had gotten accustomed to living here."

"That doesn't mean I like it." Kathleen lifted a spoonful of mashed potatoes. This time she had almost gotten it right. She added more butter and pepper.

"Hmmm." Kathleen could see the wheels turning in Joe's brain. She was learning to wait to give him the time he needed to think before pressing him for an answer. "What will happen to the manse?"

"The church can go back to using it for meetings."

"Maybe, or …" Joe rested his chin on his hand as he thought. "Or, maybe we could get an intern now that we have a place where they can live."

"Perfect. All settled. He can take over some of your workload." Katherine sliced off a bite of pork chop. Was it possible — the food was palatable? Was she becoming an okay cook? Maybe this was part of embracing her inner two on the Enneagram, learning how to care for her husband?

"Not so fast. It's not that easy. If I get an intern, I'll have to spend time supervising him or her."

"I don't care what it takes. I want out of here." Kathleen let Joe rumble around in his mind thinking through pros and cons and working out a solution while they finished dinner.

"I'll have to check with the seminary, see if they have any interns available," he said as she cleared the table. She took care of the dishes, leaving Joe to his ruminations, confident of the outcome.

Chapter 48

There wasn't much to move in. They had no furniture of their own. It all belonged to the church. Her mom and Peter had left most of their furniture.

"New furniture for a new home, a new life," her mom had said.

Mom and Peter had moved into a two-bedroom one story on the grounds of the retirement community. They had a living room and kitchen — if they felt like using it — or they could have meals in the community dining room. They could age in place, moving from their current home to assisted living when they needed more help.

"But that won't be for a long time," her mom insisted. There were activities and a new group of friends to relate to. And when they went on their long-postponed trips, they wouldn't have to worry about their home. They didn't have to worry about anything. Cleaning services were provided every other week and there was no upkeep on their home or yard.

"Just some flower beds to tend to," Peter said, then added, "if we want."

Kathleen had expected, wanted, her grandpop to stay with them, but he had plans of his own.

"You aren't the only ones ready for a change," he had told her. "I'm moving into a one-bedroom apartment in the main building. Who knows? I just might find a girlfriend."

"Grandpop!" Kathleen had laughed.

"With the ratio of men to women, you could get two or three," Joe joked.

"Yes, I hear the rumor of a new eligible bachelor has spread quickly through the community. Get ready for a few casseroles," Peter told him.

The only resident remaining was Scott, who only came out of the basement long enough to go to work then to Alex's.

"Seems funny, not having Mom or Grandpop around," Kathleen had commented their first night alone together in their new home and new bed — the one purchase they had made.

"I'm sure we could find some elderly church members who would be willing to move in."

Kathleen laughed and hit him with a pillow.

The one item they made sure to move was their Christmas fir. They picked out a place for it in their backyard, one that wouldn't interfere with random football, baseball or badminton games, then dug a hole.

Kathleen stood back and watched Joe lower the roots into the ground then drown it with water.

When done, they stood back and admired their handiwork.

"There, now it's our home," Joe said.

"Yes, it is," Kathleen responded and moved closer into the crook of his arm, safely home.

"Someday we'll have grandkids playing in the yard," Joe added. "But not too soon."

"Right, not too soon."

Kathleen had had enough changes for this year. She didn't need any more.

Chapter 49

Julia and Henry walked out of the church holding hands and laughing as a breeze blew Julia's veil off her head and picked up her skirt. She didn't have a full skirt and long train. Just a simple white dress with princess bodice that flowed over her baby bump.

Joe officiated at the service. The Catholic Church had rules about such things.

"The priest said nine months for marriage prep. He wouldn't marry us while I was pregnant. Something about it being grounds for an annulment based on coercion. Like I was coercing Henry to marry me."

"Quite the opposite. It was I who needed to coerce Julia to agree to marry me and save her from being a 'fallen woman'."

"Fortunately, we had connections to a local Lutheran pastor who was willing to do the job without a nine-month waiting period," Julia laughed.

"We Lutheran pastors have rules, too. I usually require a six-month waiting period and marriage prep. For you two, I made an exception."

It was a small wedding, barely fifty people, as befitting the situation. Family and close friends. Some of the doctors from the hospital. There was a simple cake and punch reception in the church hall before the couple departed.

"No big, fancy gala?" Kathleen teased her friend.

"I had offered to wait until after the baby was born and she had lost her baby fat, but Julia would have none of that," Henry said.

"Why wait? This way our honeymoon can also be our babymoon," Julia laughed. "Besides, I can't take a lot of time off, so we are in a hurry to get away."

Joe and Kathleen were picking up the hall after the guests left. "I'm so happy for them," Kathleen said.

"Do you wish you were Julia and expecting a baby?" Joe asked.

"No, I'm happy the way it is, happy to be with you."

"Just you and me, kid," Joe remarked, then saw Stephanie slip into the church hall. "Stephanie, we didn't know you were coming home. Is something wrong?"

"Scott told me you would be here," she walked slowly as if deciding whether to run the other way or not.

"What's wrong?" Joe asked.

"Maybe you should sit down," Stephanie said. Joe and Kathleen pulled out chairs from a table and sat down and braced themselves. Now what, Kathleen wondered? What else will she put her dad through?

"Dad, Kathleen, I'm pregnant."

Kathleen had her answer.

Chapter 50

"Now, isn't this everything I told you it would be?" Finally, Peter had gotten Esther to go away on a cruise.

"Yes, it is. I don't understand what took us so long to do this," Esther smiled at Peter. She knew far too well what, or who, had held things up. Her stubbornness, her unwillingness to admit her family wouldn't fall apart without her, her need to be needed. One blessing that had come out of her stroke was that she finally had to allow others to take care of her. She finally realized she was not indispensable. She regretted taking so long, making Peter wait, but she would make it up to him now. This was just the first of many trips they would take together.

They were cruising along the coast of Alaska, a bucket list item for Peter. She was able to maneuver about the boat with her cane, had her walker that doubled as a chair for longer walks. They would take it easy, enjoy the time they had.

They were sitting on the deck, enjoying the view of the shore and sharing a glass of champagne.

"This is the life. I'm so glad you finally talked me into doing this, Peter," Esther said as she sipped her champagne and gazed at the horizon. When Peter didn't answer, she glanced over at him. Something wasn't right. He wasn't responding. He was slumped in his chair.

"Peter, Peter …" she cried out!

Suddenly her stroke, with all of its consequences, was the last thing on her mind. Had it become the unwelcome prelude to yet another passage in her life?

Scripture Quotes Related to Suffering

Rom. 8:18 – "I consider that the sufferings of this present time are not worth comparing with the glory about to be revealed to us."

2 Cor. 12:10 – "Therefore I am content with weaknesses, insults, hardships, persecutions, and calamities for the sake of Christ; for whenever I am weak, then I am strong."

2 Cor. 1:4-7 – "Who consoles us in our affliction, so that we may be able to console those who are in any affliction with the consolation with which we ourselves are consoled by God. For just as the sufferings of Christ are abundant for us, so also our consolation is abundant through Christ. If we are being afflicted, it is for your consolation and salvation; if we are being consoled, it is for your consolation, which you experience when you patiently endure the same sufferings that we are also suffering. Our hope for you is unshaken; for we know that as you share in our sufferings, so also you share in our consolation."

2 Cor. 12 9 – "But he said to me, 'My grace is sufficient for you, for power is made perfect in weakness.' So, I will boast all the more gladly of my weakness, so that the power of Christ may dwell in me." (2 Cor. 12 is a biographical passage about St. Paul.)

Psalm 31:12, 14 – "I have passed out of mind like one who is dead; I have become like a broken vessel … But I trust in you, O Lord; I say, 'Your are my God.'"

Isaiah 63:9b – "In all their distress. It was no messenger or angel but his presence that saved them."

194

Discussion Questions

1. Victor Frankl, in his book, *Man's Search for Meaning*, states there are three ways to find meaning in life: through relationships, work and suffering. How does Esther find meaning in her life? How does that change throughout the course of the book? How do you find meaning in your life?

2. Read over the previous list of Scripture Quotes related to Suffering. Do any speak to you? Why? How does one find meaning through suffering?

3. The apple doesn't fall far from the tree, except for when it does. How does this saying hold true for Esther's relationship with her mother? Does it hold true for Kathleen's relationship with Esther? How? Does it hold true in your own relationships?

4. Esther and Kathleen attend a healing service in the book. The healing they receive is not physical healing, but emotional and spiritual. What has been your experience of healing in your life?

5. Esther and Kathleen are both going through life changes, affecting their sense of identity. Think about times that you have undergone similar changes. What helped you adjust to these changes?

6. Ashley expresses her feelings in regards to the losses in her life through dance and thereby finds some healing. Have you found healing through the arts (music, dance, pictures, sculpture, writing, movies, etc.)?

7. Esther is told she needs to find a new normal. What is this new normal? What is normal for you?

Note to the Reader

Did you enjoy reading this book? If so, please leave a review. Your comments would be appreciated and mean so much to me in terms of helping others notice my book. You, the reader, have the power to make or break a book in this day of emarketing and social media.

Thank you so much for reading *Lyrical Dance*. Stay tuned for the next book in the series!

Patricia M. Robertson

Other Novels by Patricia M. Robertson

Dreamweavers – Dream again, wherever you are in your life.

Buying Time – Visit the peace movement during the Cold War era of Ronald Regan, SDI (Strategic Defense Initiative) and MAD (Mutually Assured Destruction).

Land of Deep Waters - Honduras, land of deep waters, a country torn apart by civil unrest, violence and poverty: Is it possible to go back?

Magnificent Failure - Is it possible to start over? Failures in the eyes of the world and their own eyes, Diane and Jake found each other.

Dancing Through Life Series

Dancing on a High Wire – What do you do when life knocks you off balance? Join Sara, Joy and Esther as each seeks to find a "new normal" and regain their balance on this high wire we call life.

Still Dancing - Some phone calls we love, others we hate, like the ones Pastor Joe receives from his daughter's school. Or the one Dale received at work, letting him know his wife, Joy, had fallen and was in route to the hospital by ambulance. Could her cancer be back?

A Slow Waltz - The road to healing from loss is a slow one, sometimes going backward and sideways before going forward. Sometimes the biggest barrier to healing lies within us. Join Dale, Kathleen, Ava and others as they journey to forgiveness and healing.

An Irish Slip Step -The Irish slip jig is set in 9/8 signature time, unusual and a little off balance, like life! Kathleen didn't know about the slip jig, but she knew about slipping up. As did Chloe's, whose life was knocked off balance by an unplanned pregnancy. And then there was that fiery red-head, Mary Helen, who fell in love with an American soldier. Was it a slip-step or one of life's fortuitous missteps that brought them precisely where they were meant to be?

Delicious Secrets - Pastor Joe's church secretary retired a year ago. Since then he has struggled to find the right person to fill this position. Enter Marcie, a twenty-something college dropout, trying to find her way in the world. A church secretary was the last job she would have chosen, but she makes the best of it by entertaining herself with real and imagined secrets about church members, until she stumbles upon a secret she would rather not know. Once known, there was no turning back.

Beautiful Questions - Some questions are so big, they can take a lifetime to answer. They are big enough for you to live in, walk around in them, taste them, touch them, and test them. These are not to be taken lightly. They are beautiful questions. What are the beautiful questions in your life? Join Gwen and others as they ask beautiful questions.

About the Author

Patricia M. Robertson is an author, speaker and spiritual director, who is committed to helping individuals find God in their every day experience. She also is author of a companion non-fiction book to *Still Dancing, Walking with Families through the Dying Process*, as well as *Walking with Families through Grief,* a companion to *A Slow Waltz.*

She has written other non-fiction books and writes a weekly blog and monthly newsletter. She has a Doctor of Ministry and over thirty-five years of experience in ministry to families. She currently is enjoying her own love story with her husband, Jack, grown children and grandchildren. For more information about her ministry, go to www.patriciamrobertson.com.

Freedom Dance

Letty kicked a path through the room, littered with rags, papers, fast food wrappers, pizza boxes, and other remnants of dinners eaten in haste. She gingerly moved her booted and bandaged foot lest she slip on the rubble. The white of her cast contrasted against her warm brown skin. She lifted her right foot lest any of the debris rub against her designer shoe and noted rat droppings that warned her that live rodents couldn't be that far away.

"The building is sound. We had it inspected." Sara picked up a newspaper and tossed it aside, then wiped her paint-stained white hands on her pants. "It just needs a good cleaning."

Each room shared a similar story. A story of decay. How many homeless men and women have made this place home over the years? Had families gathered here for warmth during cold months? Letty sidestepped a pizza box.

"I saved the best for last," Sara said as she led Letty up a flight of stairs. The bar had not been set too high, Letty thought as she continued to tiptoe around mounds of waste. When they reached the landing of the stairs, Sara unlocked the chains that held double oak doors shut and opened them to display a ballroom. Overhead what appeared to be a chandelier was covered with a protective lining. Being in the innermost part of the building, the vagrants that had invaded the first floor hadn't come this far. There was still some trash in the room, a newspaper here or there, but for the most part it had been left alone.

"The chandelier is intact. We wrapped it to protect it and put the chain on the door to keep the room from any damage. This room was what sold us on the place." Sara's voice echoed through the spacious room.

Letty walked to the middle of the room and stood directly under the chandelier. She saw men and women in Civil War attire dancing about the room, the women in long, flouncy dresses, the men in suits or uniforms. Then she imagined little girls in tutus pirouetting about the floor, laughing and giggling as they danced. She saw herself, barefoot, no longer hampered by a boot, in a sleek, form fitting leotard and wrap around skirt, flying across the room, arms high, legs leaping, crinkled dark hair held back from her face with a scarf and flowing down her back. She saw potential.

Letty loved dancing with Alvin Ailey, loved New York. The two years studying with Alvin Ailey II and then three years with the actual dance troupe had been a dream come true. But what do you do after you realize a dream? Perhaps she needed a new dream. That was what she had told herself. Something had been missing. She wasn't sure what. Maybe she would find it here, in her home state. The shelf-life of a dancer was limited at best. She would be giving up some of her prime dance years if she joined this venture with Sara and her friends. She wasn't sure why she was even considering it. The right offer at the right time? Or maybe she was just ready for something different, someone different.

"So, what do you think? Are you in?" Sara asked.

Was she in? Was she ready to leave everything for a dream? Was she ready to take a chance on Detroit?

"It will work," she told Sara.

"I knew you would see what I see." Sara hugged Letty. "I've got to pick up my kids, but we'll talk more tonight."

"Will the building be ready in time for fall classes?"

"We can begin cleaning it up this weekend. We were just waiting for your approval before finalizing the deal."

"Let's do this." What was she doing, Letty thought even as she heard the words come out of her mouth.